Linda's old friend is nothing but trouble!

Linda took the shoe from Jennifer. It was a new gold shoe, now stained and dripping with hot fudge sauce. She gulped. "My mother just bought these shoes to wear to a wedding in two weeks." She held it up so that Jennifer could see. Jennifer took off the other shoe and stared at it. "They've got fudge all over them now. They look awful."

"Look, I'm sorry. But your mom can get another pair of shoes," Jennifer said, shrugging.

"My mom doesn't have that kind of money," Linda replied coolly. "If these can't be cleaned, you have to pay for another pair."

"No, I don't!" Jennifer grabbed the shoe and slammed it heel first into the top of her hot fudge sundae.

Books by Susan Smith

#9 Linda and the Little White Lies

by
Susan Smith

A MINSTREL® BOOK

PUBLISHED BY POCKET BOOKS

New York   London   Toronto   Sydney   Tokyo   Singapore

A MINSTREL PAPERBACK *ORIGINAL*

 A Minstrel Book published by
POCKET BOOKS, a division of Simon & Schuster Inc.
1230 Avenue of the Americas, New York, NY 10020

ISBN: 0-671-69454-5

First Minstrel Books printing August 1990

10 9 8 7 6 5 4 3 2 1

A MINSTREL BOOK and colophon are registered trademarks of
Simon & Schuster Inc.

Printed in the U.S.A.

For my aunt and uncle, Joan and Ceri Rees,
with love

Chapter One
❀

"Guess what, you guys!" shouted Linda Carmichael, looking down from her tree house at her best friends. Sonya Plummer, Dawn Selby, Angela King, and Monique Whitney started up the ladder.

Terri Rivera, the fifth girl, had climbed a tree next to Linda's. Now Terri grabbed a thick rope hanging from the tree and swung toward the tree house yelling, "Ahhhh" at the top of her lungs.

"Oh, no, it's Tarzetta!" exclaimed Linda. She pushed her shoulder-length blond hair behind her ears and moved back to make room for Terri.

Terri landed gracefully on the tree house platform.

The rest of the gang burst into giggles as they finished scaling the ladder to stand behind Terri.

"Okay. What's your news?" all five girls chorused.

Linda waited until everyone was quiet and seated on the wooden plank floor before continuing. "One of my old friends is coming for a visit!"

"Wow! That's great!" cried Dawn, who had been the smallest member of the group before Monique joined the gang. She leaned forward enthusiastically, blinking through her blond bangs.

"Which friend is this?" asked Sonya. She pulled a notebook out of her backpack and opened it to a clean page. Her job was to take notes for all their meetings.

"Jennifer Soo, also known as Scrap. She lives in Los Angeles, where we lived before we went to Alaska. She called and asked if she could come visit for a couple of weeks. It's okay with my parents, so she's coming."

"When does she get here?" asked Angela, wrinkling her nose against the bright sunlight. Her dark, curly hair was pulled back into two thick braids.

"Well, her school gets out earlier than ours does, so she'll be here in time for Picnic Day!" said Linda. Sixth Grade Picnic Day was the last big event of the school year. It was also the reason they were holding their meeting.

"Does she like baseball?" Monique, the girls' newest friend, asked. Monique, a year younger than the other girls, was petite and black. She looked more delicate than she really was. In spite of health problems, she was very athletic.

"Oh, yeah, sure," said Linda. "Scrap likes everything— everything I like anyway. We're just like this." She pressed two fingers together to indicate how close they were.

"It'll be fun to have someone new to show around," said Dawn, noisily crunching on some corn nuts. "Want some?" she asked everyone.

Terri thrust her hand in the bag. "Sure. Well, if she likes baseball, she's okay with me." Terri was a real sports nut. She and Linda were on a gymnastics team together, and all the girls, except Dawn, were on the Sixth Grade Picnic Day baseball team.

Linda jumped up suddenly, bumping her head on a low

branch. She rubbed the sore spot while she talked. "I can't wait to show you guys off to Scrap. I've never had so many good friends in one place before."

Linda and her family had lived all over the United States. She couldn't remember staying anywhere for more than six months at a time. That was usually because her parents would get in trouble with the law, and they'd have to move on. Since they had moved to Gladstone, Linda and her family were trying to change their images and become upstanding citizens. This was a relief to Linda because she desperately wanted a normal life.

"We are pretty wonderful," agreed Angela, drawing out the word *wonderful* dramatically. She was the actress of the group.

"Is Scrap one of your dangerous friends?" asked Dawn a little fearfully.

"Yeah, Scrap sounds like a gangster name," said Terri. "Sort of like Spike."

Linda grinned. "Well, we did get into some trouble together, but don't worry. We're both different now."

"Well, I hope so," Angela giggled.

Like her family, Linda had been in trouble for stealing when she first came to Gladstone. Making friends with Dawn had changed her life. Then she got to know Terri, Sonya, and Angela, and now they were all best friends. She knew she'd never get into trouble again.

"She wasn't named Scrap because she was a gangster, Terri," Linda informed her friend.

"Where did the name come from?" Sonya wanted to know.

"Her parents nicknamed her that when she was born, because she was such a tiny scrap of a thing," Linda said, mimicking the way Scrap had told her the story.

"Like me," said Monique.

"And me," added Dawn.

"I was in an incubator for a month," said Monique.

"I bet you wouldn't fit in one now," said Terri.

"I think Scrap is a very theatrical name," Angela told the others.

Sonya scribbled down everything in her notebook. "Oh, hey, everybody, we're supposed to be discussing Picnic Day."

"How could we forget?" Dawn flung her hand in the air and spilled her corn nuts everywhere.

"Come on. Let's go inside and get something to eat," Linda suggested as she led the way down the ladder.

"After we worked so hard to get up here," moaned Angela.

The girls trooped into the Carmichaels' huge kitchen. The interior of the ramshackle old house was being painted. At last it was beginning to look cared for. Linda gazed around the yellow kitchen, feeling pleased that her parents had decided to settle in Gladstone and fix up the house. They were renting the house with the promise that they could buy it when they came up with the down payment.

"Got any celery sticks?" asked Angela, who was always watching her weight.

Linda peered into the refrigerator. "Here you go." She handed Angela a whole celery.

"How about graham crackers and milk for the rest of us?" suggested Terri. "I'm on a graham cracker diet."

"Is that a sports diet?" asked Monique curiously. She idolized Terri.

"No, I just thought it up," Terri said.

Linda poured each girl a glass of milk, grabbed a box of graham crackers, and led the way to her bedroom.

Linda's room was covered with wall-to-wall clothes, which she almost never picked up. There were two twin beds covered with blue quilts. The girls draped themselves over the beds. Posters of gymnasts and collages of photos from everywhere Linda had lived covered the walls.

Dawn started folding Linda's clothes. "I just love this room," she said happily.

"I think we should have prizes for the sack races and relay races," Terri suggested, talking about Picnic Day again.

"We have to ask if it's okay. Maybe we'll get to pick out the prizes," said Angela.

"Do you think Scrap would like to be involved?" Dawn asked. "She could work on one of the booths or games."

"Good idea," said Linda. "I'll sign her up for something. I want her to feel part of our gang the minute she gets here."

"How did you and Scrap meet?" Dawn asked. She leaned forward to hear the story.

"Well, at the time we met my mom was driving an ice-cream truck part time, and I rode around with her sometimes," Linda explained. "We happened to stop right outside Scrap's house, and she jumped on the back of the ice-cream truck and secretly rode with us all over the neighborhood. My mom nearly died when she realized there was a kid hanging on to the back of our truck. Scrap said it was no big deal, she jumped on trucks all the time. My mom gave her an ice cream and warned her never to do it again. I loved her right away, even though she's a year younger than me, because she was crazy and wild. After that, we'd see each other every weekend until we moved."

"That's so dangerous!" exclaimed Dawn.

"Wow, what a story," said Angela. "Does she still jump on trucks?"

Linda shrugged. "I don't know. She's always been, um, adventurous, I guess you'd call her."

"She sounds like trouble," said Terri darkly.

"When we got into trouble together we found out we came from the same kind of family. Her father was in trouble for selling bad stocks," Linda said. "We only had each other to talk to about that stuff because it was so embarrassing."

"Remember when we became best friends?" Dawn asked the others.

"I'll never forget," said Sonya, looking at Angela. She and Angela had met one day by accident. Angela had thrown a mud pie that hit Sonya right in the face. Sonya began to cry, and Angela went over to apologize. From that day on they had been friends. Angela had introduced Sonya to Terri and Dawn, and the four girls had formed a bond that had remained strong ever since.

"Being friends with you guys is one of the best things that ever happened to me," Linda admitted.

"And to me," added Monique.

"And to us, too," Dawn replied, squeezing Linda's hand.

Angela, Terri, and Sonya got up and hugged Linda and Monique at the same time.

"Hey, ugh!" cried Monique between coughs. "You're smothering me!"

"Be careful! She has asthma!" Terri warned.

Simultaneously the girls released Monique, who nearly fell off the bed. She started to cough.

"Are you okay?" asked Dawn.

"Do you need water?" Angela inquired.

"Air?" asked Sonya.

"A doctor?" asked Linda, who was still being hugged by Sonya.

Monique laughed and coughed at the same time. "None of the above. You don't have to worry every time I cough or sneeze, you know. But it's nice knowing you care."

"Maybe we should have a little party for Scrap to welcome her," Angela said.

"We could go horseback riding at my house," suggested Sonya, who lived on a ranch.

"Scrap would be so impressed with that," exclaimed Linda. "She loves animals."

"We can go for a long ride and then have dinner together afterward," Sonya went on. "I'll ask my mom."

"We can make a big banner that says 'Welcome to Gladstone,' " Angela said, flopping down on a pile of pillows.

"I just love all the preparations—it's so exciting," exclaimed Dawn.

"I know you're all going to love one another." Linda said this without really knowing what Scrap was like now. It had been more than a year since they'd seen each other. When they talked on the phone they had both been so excited that they just talked about the visit.

"Once a friend, always a friend," said Dawn, gazing at her friends dreamily.

Chapter Two

At the airport on Saturday Linda stood on tiptoe to see who was coming in through the passage from the plane.

"There she is!" cried Linda, waving her hand in the air furiously as she caught a glimpse of Scrap's dark head bobbing toward her.

"Where?" asked Mrs. Carmichael.

"There!" Linda pointed at the doorway, where people were moving too slowly in a single-file line. A slight Chinese-American girl with very long, blunt-cut black hair smiled wide when she saw Linda.

Linda had recognized her right away, but she looked so different! Her new haircut and softly made-up eyes made her look so mature. She was wearing a deep purple jumpsuit with a blue sash that accentuated her slimness.

When Scrap caught sight of Linda, she wrapped the straps of her backpack around her head and waved wildly with one hand. Linda ran over and threw her arms around Scrap. Scrap wrapped her arms around Linda and dropped her bulging suitcase. It fell on Linda's foot.

"Oooh, ouch!" cried Linda, doing a little war dance. The two girls began to laugh.

"It's good to see you," said Scrap when Linda had stopped hopping.

"You look so different, Scrap. Great, but different," Linda remarked. She bent down to pick up Scrap's bag and almost didn't stand back up. "This weighs a ton. What do you carry in it, bricks?"

"No. Just my entire wardrobe," she replied, giggling.

"You would look like a model if you weren't wearing that silly pack on your head," Linda went on excitedly.

"This is the new look, Lin. Everyone must wear a backpack on her head. Haven't you been reading *Seventeen?*" teased Scrap. She posed with her hip stuck out and her hands on the pack.

"Give me a break," Linda said, laughing. She fingered the silky purple fabric of Scrap's jumpsuit. "I forgot how much you like jumpsuits. This is so pretty on you."

"Thanks. My mom bought it specially for my trip," Scrap said.

When they reached Mrs. Carmichael, she hugged Scrap warmly. "Doesn't she look like a model, Mom?"

"Yes, you're gorgeous, Scrap. The last time I saw you, you were all skin and bones," Mrs. Carmichael said.

"Do you mean I'm fat now?" Scrap asked self-consciously.

"Of course not! You're perfect," insisted Mrs. Carmichael.

"Perfect," said Linda, giving her a warm hug. "Come on. Let's get back to my house. I can't wait to show you around and introduce you to my friends—or rather, *our* friends."

Linda picked up Scrap's bag again and started walking toward the exit.

"Uh, Linda, they're not my friends," Scrap reminded her. "I don't even know them."

"Don't worry, you'll all get along just fine," said Linda with full confidence.

"I'm really a weird person, Linda," warned Scrap. She stepped in front of Linda and crossed her eyes and stuck out her tongue.

Linda just laughed. "Of course you're weird. You're my friend, aren't you?"

Mrs. Carmichael led the way to the parking lot, where they loaded the luggage and themselves into the old, beat-up dark green Chevy.

"Oh, you got a new car, I see," said Scrap jokingly.

"Yeah. I call it the Blob," Linda said. "So tell me all the gossip."

"Well, remember Mary Cavanaugh? We're best friends now," said Scrap.

"Oh, really?" asked Linda. Mary Cavanaugh had been the most popular girl at Scrap's school. She talked about her to Linda all the time. "Is she still as popular?"

"More popular, because she's become very pretty," replied Scrap proudly. "Boys love her."

"They probably never look at her when you're around," said Linda loyally.

Scrap blushed. "Oh, yes, they do!"

"Scrap, what happened to Emmy and Stacey?" asked Linda. Emmy and Stacey had been their friends.

"Oh, I never see them. Emmy moved away, and Stacey's— well, different now," said Scrap. "We don't have anything in common."

"I'm sorry," said Linda, feeling disappointed. Because she

had had to move around so much, she liked to think of other people not moving or changing.

"Hey, I brought something for you," Scrap said, digging in her backpack. She pulled out a tiny white box.

"Wow, for me?" said Linda, snatching the lid off the box eagerly. Inside, nestled against tissue paper, was a little flower pin. "Oh, it's beautiful! You know me so well. Thank you!"

When Linda picked up the pin the flower made a loud burping noise and popped out on the end of a spring.

Linda gasped, and Scrap started giggling. "Isn't it a scream?" she exclaimed. "I figured it was just right for you."

Linda fastened the brooch on her shirt and showed it to her mother.

"I've never seen anything like it," said Mrs. Carmichael.

"I can't wait to show this to the gang." Linda pressed the flower pin back into place and continued talking. "Remember the time we went sliding down the hill and your pants ripped?"

Scrap laughed. "How could I forget? Remember the time we pretended to be actresses to get into the TV studio?"

"And we were caught by the security guard right when the cameras started to roll," added Linda, shaking her head. "Wow, you have the craziest ideas."

Scrap giggled and patted Linda's hand. "Oh, by the way, nobody calls me Scrap anymore."

"Really? Why not?" asked Linda.

"Because I decided it was too immature," she explained. "My new friends call me Jennifer."

"Can I still call you Scrap?" Linda asked. "That's how I always think of you. A crazy name for a crazy person."

"I really like Jennifer better," she said.

"Well, okay," said Linda, feeling a little disappointed. She told herself that she had to get used to the idea that things change, even Scrap's name.

Mrs. Carmichael pulled into the driveway of the Carmichaels' old Victorian-style house. A big banner hung across the front of the house, which read, "Welcome to Gladstone, Scrap."

"That's really cute," said Jennifer, blushing.

"My friends and I made it—before I knew you didn't like to be called Scrap," said Linda.

"I think Jennifer is a lovely name," Mrs. Carmichael said, turning off the engine. "Now let's get you settled in, Jennifer, and have some lunch."

Jennifer gazed out the window at the shabby old house with its newly repaired front porch. "This is really your house, Linda?"

"Well, we're just renting it now. But we're going to buy it. Come on. You're sleeping in my room," she said, getting out of the car.

Scrap followed her into the house. Linda lugged the suitcase up the stairs to her room. Later they went down to the kitchen to make lunch.

Cans of paint, paint trays, and brushes were stacked up in the hallway. Newspaper was spread all over the hardwood floors.

"Please excuse the mess," Mrs. Carmichael said brightly. "We're trying to fix up the house."

"Oh, sure," said Jennifer. "We had some workmen in our house for a long time. It's a real pain."

Linda made tuna sandwiches and brought them and a bag of potato chips to the table. She ripped the bag open, and the chips flew out in all directions. One landed on Jennifer's jumpsuit.

"Oops, sorry," said Linda.

Jennifer pushed the potato chip off her lap. "The grease could stain my outfit, and they didn't have any more in my size."

Mrs. Carmichael brought some homemade spot remover over and rubbed it on the grease spot. "This should do it. It works really well."

"My mom has some great home remedies," said Linda. "She should write a book called *Mrs. Carmichael's Remarkable Remedies.*"

"I might just do it, too," said Mrs. Carmichael.

"My mother doesn't know anything like that," said Jennifer. "She leaves it to the maid."

"You have a maid?" said Linda, astonished.

"We just got one when—" Jennifer stopped and turned red. "Well, my parents just got a maid."

"Your parents got rich?" asked Linda.

"Well, sort of," replied Jennifer.

It was obvious to Linda that Jennifer didn't want to talk about it for some reason, so they finished eating in silence. Finally Linda said, "I've got to show you my tree house."

"Yippee!" yelled Jennifer.

The girls held hands as they ran out to the tree house.

"Follow me," instructed Linda, leading the way up the ladder. Jennifer grabbed hold of the rope instead and shimmied up, getting to the platform of the tree house first. Linda stared at her in amazement. "How'd you do that?"

"Watched a lot of Tarzan movies," Jennifer said, winking at her friend.

Linda shook her head. "Wow, you're just as unpredictable as I remembered. First you're worried about grease on your jumpsuit, and then you shimmy up a rope in it. That's what I love about you. I never know what you're going to do next.''

Jennifer laughed. "Neither do I. I love you because you plan things, and you're so sharp. How long did it take you to build this tree house?''

"It was here when we moved in,'' Linda explained. "I just did the decorating.''

Her friend glanced around at the gymnastics posters, the pair of painted purple high-topped sneakers hanging from a nail, and a photograph of Linda with her friends. "It looks like *Tree House Beautiful,''* Jennifer quipped. Both girls started giggling.

Linda started back down the ladder. "Come on. I'm calling my friends and asking them to come over to meet you.''

"Now, Linda?'' Jennifer asked, reaching for the rope.

Linda was already down the ladder and on her way across the yard. "Well, what's wrong with now?''

"I just thought we could spend some time together first,'' Jennifer said, sliding down the rope.

"We can—before they get here,'' said Linda. She went inside to dial Terri's number.

Within an hour Terri, Dawn, Angela, and Sonya arrived on Linda's doorstep. Monique hadn't been able to come.

Terri had on a leotard top with jeans pulled on over it. "I came right away and didn't take time to change after my workout.''

Sonya and Angela pinched their noses. "Hold your noses, everyone!''

"Don't listen to them,'' said Terri. "I'm Terri, and I don't smell.''

Dawn spoke at almost the same time. "I'm Dawn.''

"I'm Sonya, and this is Angela," said Sonya. Now there were four names for Jennifer to remember.

"Uh, are you ready to pass the quiz on their names?" Linda asked, teasing her friend.

Jennifer smiled and repeated each girl's name perfectly. "I'm really happy to meet you all."

"Us, too," said Dawn. "How do you like Gladstone so far, Scrap?"

"Fine, but I've only been here about an hour," she said, looking at Linda.

"Look what Scrap—I mean Jennifer—gave me, you guys," said Linda, pointing to her flower pin.

"Oooh!" exclaimed Dawn. She reached out and touched the flower, and it popped out at her.

Everyone gasped. "Wow, what a neat gift," said Angela.

The four girls bustled into the house and immediately went up to Linda's room. "I've got something for a special treat," said Linda. She disappeared downstairs and returned a minute later with a plate of freshly made cinnamon rolls.

A cry of "Mmmm!" rose from all the girls.

"My mom made these just for you, Scr—Jennifer," said Linda, offering her friend one.

"Thanks, Linda," said Jennifer. "You and your mom are already spoiling me to death. In fact, I'm going to get fat with all this food."

Linda offered the cinnamon rolls to everyone, then settled down on the carpet. "This is a special occasion. We don't eat like this all the time."

"Do you remember the time we stole cinnamon rolls from a bakery and they were so hot, you had to juggle them as we ran down the street?" asked Jennifer.

"You stole cinnamon rolls from a bakery?" asked Dawn in horror.

Linda blushed. "Before I knew you. Dawn's family owns a wonderful bakery."

"Oh, sorry," said Jennifer. "Oh, and how about the time we stole all those chocolate bars at the movies?"

Linda was obviously feeling uncomfortable. "We got caught, though, remember?"

Jennifer started laughing. "They called our parents, and we were grounded for a month and barred from that theater."

"Did you think getting caught with stolen candy bars was fun?" asked Terri.

"It wasn't fun at all," Jennifer said sharply. "It was just something Linda and I shared. Just about the time Linda left town I got caught stealing record albums, and after that I stopped stealing. It's not a good experience—Lin can tell you that, too. We're okay now, though, aren't we, Lin?" She linked arms with her friend.

Linda nodded. No one but Jennifer had ever called her "Lin."

Angela, Sonya, Terri, and Dawn were quiet and just listened to the two girls. Linda changed the subject quickly.

"Scrap likes to be called by her real name—Jennifer—now," said Linda.

"Oh," said Sonya.

"Well, hi, Jennifer," said Angela, smiling warmly. "I understand that. Some people used to call me Fatso, but I'm glad I outgrew that name."

"*You?* I can't believe it. You're so thin," said Jennifer, looking Angela up and down.

"Angela's got the most self-control of anyone I know,"

said Sonya proudly. "She went on a diet, and she's looked great ever since."

"She always looked great," corrected Dawn. "But I understand why you wanted to change your name, too. Terri liked to call me Pinhead, but I think I've outgrown that name now," she added with a quick glance at Terri.

"Dawn went down to L.A. recently with her family, and they were on 'Family Fortune,' " said Linda. "They won."

"Really? Congratulations. That's one of my favorite shows," exclaimed Jennifer. "I'd love to go on that show. If only my father didn't work for a studio."

"Your father works for the *studios?*" said Dawn, very impressed.

"Well, yes. He's a screenwriter at one of the biggest studios," replied Jennifer.

The girls gasped.

"Would we know any of his movies?" asked Sonya, who loved glitzy movie gossip.

"He does made-for-TV movies, like *Man with a Rifle, Bankroll,* and *Western Omelet,* said Jennifer. She stood up on a chair and balanced on one foot.

"Oh, I loved *Western Omelet,* " exclaimed Dawn. "About the omelet that just ran amok and took over an entire town. I can't believe this. So this means that you actually *know* celebrities?"

"Well, yeah," said Jennifer as if it was nothing important.

Sonya took a small bite of her cinnamon roll. "Do you know Craig Lightman?"

"My dad and I had dinner with him just the other night," said Jennifer, beaming. Now she had all the girls' attention.

"I just *love* him. He's my hero," said Angela, sighing dramatically.

"What about Bobby Chieftain?" asked Sonya.

"He lives down the street from me," said Jennifer.

"Oh, this is *so* exciting!" exclaimed Dawn. She was so excited that she jumped up and stepped on a cinnamon roll.

"You've got cinnamon roll oozing between your toes," yelled Terri. "How gross!" Everyone started laughing.

Dawn pulled off the stepped-on part of the cinnamon roll and pretended to eat it. "Now that is *really* gross!" said Sonya.

"What about Sal Brio?" asked Angela after Dawn cleaned up her foot.

"Oh, my best friend knows him," said Jennifer, flopping down onto one of the chair arms.

"Maybe you could invite somebody famous to come to Picnic Day," suggested Linda. "Everyone would be so impressed."

"When is it?" Jennifer asked.

"Tomorrow," Linda said.

Jennifer shook her head. "I don't know anyone who could come on such short notice. They're all so busy, you know."

Linda stood up to make an announcement. "We have big plans for the rest of today—horseback riding at Sonya's house!"

"Afterward we're all going to have dinner at my house. It's fine with my mom," said Sonya excitedly.

"That's really nice of you," said Jennifer politely.

After Linda and Jennifer had changed into jeans Mrs. Carmichael drove the girls over to Sonya's. Six horses were saddled and waiting outside the barn. Sonya's stepfather, Bob Stretch, helped the girls into their saddles.

He winked at Jennifer. "I just knew it. You're even prettier than Linda said you'd be."

Jennifer blushed, and the girls laughed.

"Don't mind him," Sonya said as they were riding along the trail. "He teases all my friends."

"He's nice," said Jennifer. "You're lucky to live on a ranch."

"Sonya didn't think so at first," said Linda as they rode through a dry creekbed. "She lived in New York City for a year with her father before moving down to the ranch."

"I wasn't sure I'd like living out here," Sonya explained. "It seems so far from everything, but now I love it. And it is only fifteen minutes from town."

They rode up to the top of a mountain and watched a hawk circle high above a distant pine ridge. They slowly made their way along the trail back to the ranch. When they were within sight of the house, Jennifer stood up on her saddle and stretched her arms out for balance.

"Jennifer, get down!" exclaimed Linda in horror. "You could hurt yourself."

Sonya turned around and looked at her. "Oh, no! What if the horse gets spooked? Get down!"

Jennifer giggled like a maniac but did as the girls suggested. "It did look great, though, didn't it?"

Linda rode up beside her. "Why did you do that? You scared me half to death!"

"I took lessons from a movie stuntman," she explained. Then out of the blue she clutched her heart and slumped forward in her saddle, as though she'd been hit by a bullet or something.

"Jen, are you all right?" cried Linda. Everyone else turned to look, too. Jennifer raised her head and grinned.

"Hey, I fooled you, didn't I? I really looked dead, didn't I?"

"Yes!" the girls chorused.

"I learned that from the stuntman, too," she said proudly.

"You shouldn't ever pretend to be hurt or dead," said Dawn worriedly. "You'll end up like the little boy who cried 'wolf.'"

"Nah," said Jennifer. "It's all just for fun."

When they returned to the house, Mrs. Stretch and Bob Stretch, Sonya's mom and stepdad, were out in the backyard barbecuing ribs. A wooden picnic table was set up with potato salad, green salad, and French bread. Monique had arrived and Linda introduced her to Jennifer. Then she and Sonya went inside to get the silverware and dishes.

Bob brought a huge platter of ribs to the table, and everyone except Jennifer dug in.

"Bob makes the best barbecued ribs," said Linda.

"This side of the Mississippi," he added, winking at her.

"You know, Mr. Stretch, these ribs are as good as my grandma's, and that's saying something," Monique announced.

"Well, I'll be," Bob Stretch said, shaking his head in amazement.

"Aren't you eating any?" Terri asked Jennifer.

She was picking at a tiny sparerib. "I'm not all that hungry," she said.

"It's all that flying and horseback riding," said Mrs. Stretch comfortingly. "You don't have to eat if you don't want to, dear."

After dinner Linda brought out a huge chocolate sheet cake with "Welcome, Scrap" written across it.

"Oh, you shouldn't have done that," cried Jennifer, her eyes round and full of tears.

"We wanted to," said Dawn.

Monique sighed very loudly and long. "I can't have any—I'm allergic to chocolate, unfortunately. I'm also allergic to horses. That's why I couldn't come riding today," she explained to Jennifer.

"Oh, no, I feel so guilty eating this," said Dawn, staring at her piece of cake.

Sonya disappeared into the house and came out with a slice of white cake. She put in down in front of Monique.

"Here you go. Just for you."

Monique sampled the thin slice of cake Sonya offered her. "It's very good. Thank you, but I'm going to pretend it's chocolate," she said.

Terri pushed herself away from the table first. "Okay, now I'm ready for some way to work off all that food."

Linda didn't say anything but disappeared for a minute. When she came back she had badminton rackets, which she handed around. "Will this do?" she asked Terri. Terri nodded. "Come on, Jennifer. Let's show them how to play."

Jennifer balanced a racket on the end of her nose.

"Hey, that's really impressive for starters," said Angela. "Can you teach me how to do that?"

"Oh, sometime, sure." Then she turned to Linda and whispered, "I'm really too tired to play badminton right now," she insisted. "I'd like to go home, if you don't mind, Linda."

Terri, who never wasted time where sports were involved, and the others were already playing.

Linda was puzzled by Jennifer. She had never known her to leave a party early, especially one for her.

"I guess you must be really tired," she said to Jennifer. "I'll call my mom and have her pick us up."

After Linda went inside and called her mother, she told her friends that they were going home.

"You're leaving?" said Dawn. All the girls stopped playing badminton to stare at Jennifer and Linda.

"Uh, Jennifer's tired," said Linda.

"Hey, we'll see you tomorrow at Picnic Day, Jennifer," said Terri. "We've got plans for you."

Jennifer's eyes widened with curiosity. "Oh, really?"

Soon Mrs. Carmichael was out front honking her car horn.

"My mom's here," said Linda. Reluctantly, she waved goodbye to her friends. She felt disappointed with Jennifer, and Linda wasn't convinced that Jennifer was really tired.

Chapter Three

⚘

The next morning Linda tried on half a dozen outfits for Picnic Day. Finally she chose a pair of stone-washed pink jeans and a shocking-pink shirt.

"What's the big deal?" asked Jennifer, who was lounging on her twin bed.

"It's the biggest event of the school year—and the last," explained Linda. "I want to look good."

"But you're playing baseball," she said. "You'll get all dirty."

"I know," said Linda, peeling off the jeans. "I'll take these with me for later."

Suddenly the phone rang. Linda ran to answer it.

"Linda? It's Monique. I'm sick. I have a code in my doze," she said stuffily.

"You sound like you have a clothespin on your nose," Linda said.

"My father won't allow me to play. If it was up to me—" Monique began.

"Yes, I know. If it was up to you, you'd play even if you had pneumonia," said Linda.

"I was wondering if Scrap—er, Jennifer—could play in my place," said Monique.

"I'm sure she'd love to," said Linda. "Can we come by and see you after Picnic Day?"

"Sure, but you'd better stay far away from me. I'm contagious," warned Monique.

"What are you volunteering me for?" asked Jennifer. She had sat bolt upright on the bed when she heard her name.

Linda hung up the phone. "Monique's sick, and she thought you'd like to take her place on our baseball team."

"And you said I would without asking me," said Jennifer huffily.

"You always loved to play baseball," insisted Linda. "Did you stop loving it or something?"

"I just don't want to get my clothes messed up," she replied. Her blue print jumpsuit wasn't made for baseball.

"Since when did you get so prissy?" asked Linda.

Jennifer stuck her hands on her hips indignantly. "I am not 'prissy,' as you call it."

Linda whistled through her teeth. "Change into some shorts, like me. Come on, dummy, we have to go." She half folded her jeans and shirt before stuffing them into a tote bag. Then she tossed in a white shirt and red shorts for Jennifer, who wore a size smaller than she did. "By the time we get there you'll have changed your mind."

Linda stopped in the kitchen to pick up the brownies her mom had made for the picnic.

Reluctantly, Jennifer wheeled Linda's bike out to the street behind Linda, who was riding her brother Jon's bike.

Jennifer sounded panicky when she said, "I don't want to ride out in the street where there are cars."

"We'll go along the dirt road to the park, then," said Linda, trying to keep the irritation out of her voice.

The two girls pedaled as fast as they could down the dirt path. Linda loved the way the wind pulled her long hair straight out behind her. She felt wonderful in the morning warmth, riding through the dappled sunshine under a canopy of trees.

Jennifer whooped with joy. Suddenly she passed Linda with her arms folded across her chest. "Look, Ma—no hands!" she yelled as she whizzed ahead.

"Be careful!" Linda yelled up to her, but she couldn't help laughing. Racing with Jennifer reminded her of their reckless old times.

Within a few minutes they had reached the park, and Jennifer crossed onto the grass two bike lengths ahead of her friend.

As they flew across the lawn, Linda saw Dawn waving her arms wildly and Terri running toward them.

"Monique called you, didn't she?" Terri asked. Linda nodded. "Are you going to help us, Jennifer?" Terri asked as Jennifer braked, throwing herself into a crazy spin.

Sonya and Angela ran over to join them.

"I really don't want to," replied Jennifer, shaking her head.

"Oh, please! We need you!" cried Sonya.

"Come on, Jennifer. I brought extra clothes for you," said Linda.

Jennifer turned to her, her gaze hot and angry. "I told you I didn't want to play, Linda."

Linda held up her hands. "And I think you're just being prissy." The two girls glared at each other.

"Well, all right. I'll play," said Jennifer.

"Hurrah!" yelled all the girls.

"All right." Terri clamped her cap on her head and threw Jennifer a catcher's mitt. "Let's go."

Jennifer hurried after Terri, Sonya, and Angela.

The game between the Maniacs (Tommy Atwood's team) and the Wildcats (Terri's team) began. Terri was pitching, Jennifer was catching, Angela was playing first, and Dawn, who had been convinced to play because other kids dropped out, was between second and third. Sonya and Linda were in the field. The first batter struck out. The second batter was Tommy, who made it to first but got greedy and tried for second. Linda and Dawn ran him down and tagged him out between first and second. The third batter hit a fly ball, which Sonya easily caught.

"Batter up!" yelled Terri at Sonya. She tossed the ball to Tommy, who was pitching for his team.

Linda pushed Sonya forward. "Hey, you're up."

"Go, Sonya!" yelled Angela.

Linda, Dawn, and Terri also shouted encouragement to Sonya from the bench. On the third pitch, with two strikes against her, Sonya whacked the ball so hard it sailed high over the outfielders' heads. A hush fell over the bleachers as everyone watched the ball's slow arc. Then as Sonya started to run around the bases everyone began screaming.

"Go, Sonya, go, Sonya!" yelled her best friends.

Linda glanced up at the bleachers. Howard Tarter, who was dressed in the Gladstone Gopher mascot suit, was clapping loudly for Sonya and jumping up and down. As Sonya crossed home plate Howard bounded down the bleachers to give her a big, furry hug.

"How romantic!" said Angela, and she sighed.

"You're up, Jennifer," said Terri.

Jennifer took her place at bat and struck out. Linda was

really surprised. Jennifer had been one of those people who could always hit the ball. The game ended with a score of three to nothing—the Wildcats' favor. The girls all whooped and leaped, screaming with excitement.

When everyone calmed down, Jennifer left the group and headed for a crowd of boys standing by the bleachers. As the girls were walking back to their bench, Sonya pointed toward the bleachers. "Look at Jennifer."

Linda looked up at her friend. Jennifer was balancing on the wooden rail that surrounded the bleachers with boys surrounding her, clapping.

"And look over there," said Sonya, motioning toward Celia Forester, the prettiest and snobbiest girl in the sixth grade. She was standing with her two friends, Jeannie Sandlin and Polly Clinker, glaring at Jennifer.

"Uh-oh. Celia's jealous," said Linda, grinning.

"She thinks all boys are her personal property," Sonya said. "Now she's got competition."

Linda pulled her hair into a ponytail. "She always had us," she said with determination.

Everyone watched as Jennifer grabbed the rail with her hands and swooped down to meet her all-male audience.

Howard began to dance in a circle around Jennifer.

"What's he doing?" Sonya asked out loud, her face growing red. Howard was her boyfriend.

Linda shrugged. "Now don't get mad. You know how crazy Howard is."

"He just better not be crazy about *her,*" said Sonya huffily.

Linda and the others trooped over to the boys.

Jennifer flashed them a big smile.

The girls smiled back.

"I was just showing everyone how to balance on something

skinny and telling them about the studio where my father works,'' Jennifer said.

''I've never met a real celebrity before,'' said Lyle Kraus, a boy who had a crush on Dawn. After Dawn and her family won on ''Family Fortune,'' he had gotten into the habit of following Dawn everywhere.

''You know me, Lyle,'' said Terri, who was a good gymnast.

''And me,'' said Dawn.

Lyle turned bright pink. ''Oh, well, you guys are different.''

''Did you learn to balance in gymnastics?'' asked Dawn.

''No, I learned from a stuntman. He taught me how to walk a tightrope. I can teach you how,'' said Jennifer.

Dawn shivered. ''No, thank you.''

''Hey, it's time for the sack race,'' said Linda, turning to go.

Everyone followed her, still talking.

Linda, Terri, Angela, Dawn, and Sonya stepped into sacks and held them up around their thighs. They hopped up to the chalk starting line.

Jennifer, trailing her sack behind her, said, ''Linda, I think I'll sit and watch.''

''Come on, Jen. It'll be fun,'' urged Linda.

Jennifer shook her head. ''Not this time.''

There wasn't time to argue. Mrs. Montgomery, the supervisor of the race, came over and stood next to the girls.

She yelled, ''Ready, set—go!'' Everyone leapt forward.

Linda hopped forward clumsily, trying to keep her balance. Next to her was a cute boy she hadn't ever seen before. His straight, reddish-brown hair flopped over his eyes as he hopped. Freckles dotted his arms and face. When he turned to face her, he grinned.

Linda smiled. Then she turned away, determined not to let herself be distracted by him. She hopped as hard as she could, taking giant leaps. They reached the top of a small, grassy hill. At the bottom the race would end. Going down on the far side, Linda was still going at the same speed. She couldn't stop herself. Inside the sack she was hopping around crazily, trying to avoid falling down. Right behind her she heard laughter. It blew her concentration, and she lost her balance and tumbled down the far side of the hill.

She heard the boy behind her fall, too. He rolled and laughed, rolled and laughed. Linda saw the finish line only fifteen feet ahead and rolled toward it. Just as she passed over it the boy with red hair and freckles rolled on top of her.

"It's a tie!" cried Mrs. Montgomery, waving a red flag in the air.

Linda and the boy stood up, and their sacks fell down around their ankles. The boy threw his arms around her. Surprised, Linda hugged him back.

"Congratulations!" she shouted in his ear.

"Same to you!" he replied. "Hey, I'm Zack. What's your name?"

Linda was sure her heart had stopped beating. "Linda."

"Where do you go to school?" asked Linda.

"Next year I'll be going to Banner Junior High," he replied.

"Me, too!" Linda exclaimed. "Hey, what're you doing in the Gladstone sack race?"

At that moment Mrs. Montgomery stepped over to the two of them and slipped a gold-painted medal threaded onto a blue ribbon around each one's neck. "Congratulations, Linda and—what's your name?"

"Zack," he said. When she left he whispered in Linda's ear, "Just between you and me, I'm with another school group—over there. I shouldn't be a winner in this sack race."

Linda grinned. "Are you going to let me be the winner all by myself?"

"Sure," he said, stepping all the way out of his sack. Then he slipped his medal over Linda's head.

Just then some boys yelled and waved at him. "Hey, Zack! Over here!"

Zack waved back. "Well, Linda—I guess I'll see you in junior high."

Linda opened her mouth to say something, but he was already running to rejoin his group.

"Who was that hunk?"

Linda turned around to see Jennifer grinning at her. "His name is Zack, and he's going to my school next year."

"Lucky you," said Jennifer.

"I just hope I don't have to wait until junior high to see him again," Linda said, sighing.

"I think he likes you," Jennifer said.

Terri, Angela, Sonya, and Dawn were still in their sacks and hopping. They bounced over to congratulate Linda on her win.

"This is exhausting," said Angela breathlessly. She leaned against Sonya, who got off balance and grabbed for Dawn to steady herself. All three girls collapsed on the grass, laughing.

"Congratulations on winning the sack race," said Dawn.

"I saw that cute boy you rolled across the line with," said Sonya, winking at Linda.

Linda blushed. "It was a tie, but Zack gave me his medal because he doesn't go to Gladstone and couldn't legally accept it." She displayed both medals for everyone to see.

"Oh, it's 'Zack,' is it?" teased Sonya. "Like you've known him for years."

"I'm impressed," said Terri. "Now let's get some food." Lunch had just been announced. The girls returned their sacks to Mrs. Montgomery. Terri led the way to the food tables.

"Later today let's go visit Monique," suggested Dawn. The girls piled their plates high with all the food the parents had fixed.

Angela carefully removed the bun from her hot dog and ate it plain.

Much later, just as the girls were getting ready to go, Angela said, "I want to do the balloon toss before we leave."

"Me, too!" cried Sonya.

The girls marched over to the balloon toss. Each took a turn throwing darts at balloons that were pinned to a board. Jennifer tried it but was unable to hit any balloons. She aimed at the stuffed-animal prizes instead, and Eddie Martin, who was working there, took the darts away from her. The other girls were surprised at her behavior. Sonya hit six balloons and won a tiny stuffed puppy.

Before leaving, Dawn wrapped some cookies in a napkin for Monique. Then all six girls got on their bikes and rode the short distance to Monique's house. When they arrived Monique's little brother, Barry, let them in.

"Monique is sicker than a dog," he announced. "You don't want to get anywhere near her."

He led the way along the tile hallway to Monique's bedroom. Monique's tiny face peered out from amid a clutter of tissue boxes, cold medicines, and blankets.

"Hi," she croaked, managing a smile.

"Hi," everyone shouted.

Jennifer stared at the walls of the bedroom. Posters of base-ball heroes, Olympic gold medalists, and the first woman astronaut filled every available wall space.

"I guess you're really into sports," said Jennifer.

"Yes, I play anything my father lets me. He's very protec-tive of me, you know," Monique said. She sneezed. "More than anything, I want to be brave."

"You are brave," insisted Terri. Monique beamed at her.

While the others were talking Jennifer stuck tissues up her nose and in her ears and taped them above her eyebrows. Then she turned around to face Monique. "Ta-da!" she cried, holding her arms out.

"What in the world?" asked Linda.

Monique giggled hysterically, and all the other girls joined in.

Dawn handed Monique the napkin filled with cookies, which were now only crumbs. "Here, I brought these for you. Sorry about how mashed they are."

"Oh, thank you. They look delicious," said Monique, popping some crumbs into her mouth.

"You're actually going to *eat* those?" asked Jennifer, look-ing disgusted.

"Sure I am. Dawn brought them to me, and they're good. Want some?" Monique offered. She sneezed again.

"No, thanks," said Jennifer, walking toward the door. "I'm going to wait outside."

"With all those tissues stuck to your face?" asked Terri. Everyone giggled as they watched her yank the tissues from her face.

Linda turned and watched Jennifer leave the room.

"What's wrong with her?" asked Terri. "Sometimes she's a lot of fun, and other times—well, she's kind of whiny."

Linda shrugged. "She used to be fun more often. Maybe she's upset about something."

"Like what? She had all the sixth-grade boys going nuts over her today," Angela pointed out.

"That doesn't necessarily make a person happy," Dawn said.

"How would you know, Pinhead? You don't even like boys," said Terri, teasing her.

"Right. But I decided I don't like being called 'Pinhead,' either," Dawn reminded her.

"Sorry, Shrimp," said Terri.

"It's hard to be the new person in a group," said Linda.

"Yeah. Maybe Jennifer's feeling funny about that," suggested Sonya.

"Maybe. Hey, thanks for being understanding, you guys," Linda told them. "You're the best."

"We are, aren't we?" Dawn piped up cheerfully.

Linda decided she'd make an extra effort to understand Jennifer. Maybe they needed to get to know each other all over again.

Chapter Four

Linda's parents were in the kitchen making dinner when Linda and Jennifer arrived home that day.

"Indian food," exclaimed Linda, sniffing the fragrant air in the front hall. "As I'm sure you remember, my mom and dad are great cooks. Let's go see what they're making."

"No, thanks. I don't like Indian food," said Jennifer, but she did follow Linda into the kitchen.

"Hi, girls!" called Mr. and Mrs. Carmichael. They were both wearing aprons and leaning over the stove.

Linda's tall seventeen-year-old brother, Jon, was in the kitchen, sitting at the table. "What's this?" he asked, looking over at Jennifer. He pushed his long brown hair out of his eyes. "Did I hear you say you don't like Indian food?"

She blushed prettily. "Actually, I've never tried it."

"You must." Jon took a wooden spoon and dipped it into a pot that was simmering on top of the stove.

"It's very hot, Jon," warned Mrs. Carmichael, wiping her spice-stained hands on her apron.

Jennifer tasted the chicken mixture, wrinkling her nose.

"Like it?" Jon asked, and he put the spoon in the sink.

"It's good, but spicy," she answered, dabbing her mouth with a napkin.

"And on the back burner we have dyed shirts," said Linda, lifting a shirt out of dripping dye with a big fork. "Want a taste?"

"We're dyeing shirts for silk-screening," explained Mr. Carmichael. "It's our new business venture."

"It's kind of messy," observed Jennifer, noting the pale blue puddles on the stove top.

"But it's fun," Linda told her. "Some things are messy but fun." She was feeling irritated with the way Jennifer was behaving.

While Linda set the table, Jennifer sat and read a fashion magazine.

"Aren't you going to help me?" asked Linda, clunking the silverware down noisily.

"You do it so well, Linda, you don't need me," she replied.

"Yes, I do. I could use some help," Linda grumbled. Reluctantly, Jennifer got up to help.

After dinner Linda and Jon cleared the table and put the dishes in to soak. Jennifer sat watching them.

"Don't you do chores at home?" asked Linda.

"No, we have a maid, remember?" Jennifer told her.

"I'd love a maid," said Jon. "Someone to put on my slippers and bring me my dinner." He flopped into a chair.

"Ours is a really good cook," said Jennifer. "And our maid is the cousin of Tulip Winthrop, the movie star. You know who she is, don't you, Jon?"

"Do I? She's gorgeous! I'd love to meet her in person!" he exclaimed.

"She's really nice," said Jennifer, sighing dramatically.

"The best part about having a maid is that I don't have to do anything around the house."

"Except make messes," added Linda, gazing at the sea of half-eaten cookies in front of Jennifer. "I bet you've become an expert mess maker."

Jennifer smiled brightly, then turned and batted her eyelashes at Jon. "Let's go play Scrabble or something, Lin."

"When I finish here," said Linda. "Or you could help, and we could get it done in half the time."

Halfheartedly Jennifer wiped the table, leaving crumbs and salad dressing stuck to the surface. Linda had to do it over again. She was ready to strangle one of her dearest friends!

The next morning Linda asked Jennifer to make some toast while she got out the cereal.

"How do you work the toaster oven?" asked Jennifer.

Linda showed her friend what to do. "Press this little button."

Jennifer followed Linda's instructions.

"Brilliant, Jennifer," said Jon, patting her shoulder.

Jennifer sat down with a cup of cocoa and forgot about the toast.

"Hey, what's burning?" Linda asked after a few minutes.

"The toast!" yelled Jon, running to the toaster oven. Armed with a potholder, he pulled open the toaster oven door.

Smoke spewed from the toaster oven in thick gray clouds, and sparks shot out from the cord. Everyone started coughing. Mr. and Mrs. Carmichael ran into the kitchen, asking what had happened.

Linda yanked the electric cord out of the outlet. "There! Everything's okay now. The toaster oven just blew up."

"It was all my fault," said Jennifer tearfully.

"Not really. Sometimes the button gets stuck," said Linda.

"I'm sure you didn't mean to blow it up," said Jon.

"No one ever intentionally blows up a toaster oven," said Mr. Carmichael reassuringly. "These things happen."

"It was old," Mrs. Carmichael added.

"Excuse me," Jennifer said, and ran upstairs. A few minutes later they all heard a crash.

"What was that?" asked Jon.

"It sounded like glass breaking," said Linda. "Maybe Jennifer broke a window."

Linda flew up the stairs to find Jennifer standing in the bathroom, staring down at a broken hand mirror.

"Now I'll have seven years' bad luck," she moaned tearfully.

Linda shrugged. "Maybe if you clean it up really fast, it won't happen."

"What happened?" asked Jon.

"I was balanced on the edge of the sink looking into the mirror like this." She demonstrated, stretching her mouth out of shape and sticking out her tongue. "I accidentally slipped and knocked the hand mirror off the counter."

"An accident looking for a place to happen," said Linda teasingly as the two girls carefully swept the jagged glass into a dustpan. "Maybe you should just stop clowning around, Jen."

"I thought that's what you liked about me," said Jennifer.

"I do and I don't," Linda replied honestly. "It would be okay if you didn't break things."

"Maybe I should go back to bed and start all over," said Jennifer.

"It's no big deal," said Jon, trudging downstairs. He flung his arms up and exclaimed, "Girls!"

Finally when all the glass was picked up, Linda went downstairs to throw it in the trash. Maybe Jennifer was just nervous about being in a strange place, she thought.

When Linda returned from school that afternoon Jennifer was waiting for her in the kitchen.

"I made us a snack," she said, grinning.

Linda smiled. Maybe Jennifer was trying to make up for the mess she'd made that morning, she considered.

Linda followed her into the kitchen to find that Jennifer had made two hot fudge sundaes.

"What a treat!" exclaimed Linda. The two girls sat down at the table.

"I'm glad you like it," said Jennifer, smiling. "I'm really sorry about the mirror."

"It's okay." Just then Linda noticed the trail of chocolaty footprints leading from the stove to the table. "Uh, Jen, look at the floor."

Jennifer looked down and gasped. "Oh, no! I didn't mean to do that!" She leapt to her feet, upsetting her sundae. It fell face-down onto her shoes.

"And you didn't mean to dump your sundae, either," said Linda, laughing. "Come on, let's clean it up."

Jennifer pushed the sundae off the shoes and walked over to the stove to get a rag. The *clump-clump* of her shoes caught Linda's attention. She looked down and noticed that Jennifer was wearing high heels.

"Those look like my mom's shoes," said Linda.

"I was just playing with them," Jennifer said defensively. She hopped on one foot to take off a shoe.

"What were you doing in my mom's room?" demanded Linda.

"I told you. Just playing around. I do it with my mom's shoes all the time," answered Jennifer.

"Yes, but that's your mom. My mom doesn't allow it," Linda insisted.

Linda took the shoe. It was a new gold-dyed satin shoe, now stained and dripping with hot fudge sauce. She gulped. "My mother just bought these shoes to wear to a wedding this weekend." She held it up so that Jennifer could see. Jennifer took off the other shoe and stared at it. "They've got fudge all over them now. They look awful."

"Look, I'm sorry. But your mom can get another pair," Jennifer said, shrugging.

"No, she can't. My mom doesn't have that kind of money," Linda replied coolly. "If these can't be cleaned, you'll have to pay for another pair."

"No, I won't!" Jennifer slammed the shoe in her hand down onto the table. Linda's hot fudge sundae flew up into the air and flipped over.

"Now look what you've done!" cried Linda. "There isn't very much time until the wedding." She rubbed at the soiled satin on the shoe she was holding with the corner of a napkin. It only made the fudge smear. She had an idea just then. "Tell you what. I'm going to find a way for you to earn the money after we clean up this mess."

"How in the world will I earn any money?" cried Jennifer, following Linda upstairs after all the traces of hot fudge were removed from the kitchen.

"I don't know yet, but I'll figure out a way." Linda went into her parents' room and found the shoe box. She placed the shoes in it. "Come on. First we're going to try a shoe repair shop. Maybe they can do something."

Linda and Jennifer walked to the shoe repair shop. The cobbler shook her head sadly after she had studied the shoes.

"Hmmm. They sure do smell good. But I'm sorry, there's nothing I can do for them. They're beyond hope," she said, putting them back in their box.

Outside the shop Linda hugged the shoe box to her chest.

"My mom has so many shoes, she wouldn't even miss one pair," said Jennifer.

"Oh, yeah? Well, if you're so rich now maybe you can get the money for a new pair of shoes from her," said Linda.

Jennifer's face drained of color. "I don't think so. No, that won't work."

On the way home Linda dropped the shoe box into the garbage can of the neighbors across the street, the Marcuses.

Jennifer watched her, looking sad. "You won't tell on me, will you, Linda? My mom and dad get super angry with me if I get into trouble."

Linda bit her lip, remembering how she had promised herself to be more understanding with Jennifer. Finally she shook her head. "No, I won't tell. But I'm getting really tired of covering up for you."

"It's just a little white lie," said Jennifer.

"It's going to be a big white lie if we don't figure out a way to get the money for another pair of shoes by Sunday," warned Linda darkly.

Chapter Five

🎔

On Tuesday morning Linda met Terri, Dawn, Angela, and Sonya outside her house.

"Only four more days of school," said Sonya. "I wonder if I'll see Howard this summer."

"We'll have to figure out ways to see everyone this summer," said Angela.

"I need a job—and fast," announced Linda. She didn't want to tell her friends about Jennifer and the shoes. "I thought maybe we could all do something to make money."

"What a good idea!" cried Sonya.

"I wonder if Zack has a paper route," said Linda as they rode single file down the road toward school. "I don't even know his last name!"

"So you can't find him in the phone book," said Terri, who was in the lead as usual.

"This is a real mystery," said Dawn.

"If you could find out his last name, you could ride past his house," suggested Angela. "That's what I did when I first liked Bobby."

Sonya giggled. "How romantic! And Bobby just happened to be outside, right?"

"It was just like in the movies," said Angela dreamily.

"I've got an idea," Linda said. "What about a big event or contest, something that we could advertise all over town? We could charge admission. That way I'd have an interesting job, and Zack could come to our—whatever—and I'd see him again."

"Sounds good," said Terri. She slowed down so she wouldn't get too far ahead of the others. "Go on."

"What kind of an event would a boy come to?" asked Linda.

"Not a fashion show," said Sonya.

"A lemonade stand?" suggested Dawn.

"No, that's for babies," replied Terri. "Something really big that will get a lot of attention."

"A play," said Angela.

"No. Plays cost too much," Sonya told her.

"I know!" Linda stepped hard on her brakes. Everyone except Sonya braked behind her. Sonya crashed into the back of Linda's bike.

"Are you okay?" asked Linda.

Sonya smiled. "Yeah, but what's your big idea?"

"A bike race."

"I love it!" cried Dawn.

"It is a great way to get every kid in town to come," said Terri.

"It's also a great way to get known in junior high," Sonya added. "Just think! Everyone will remember us as the girls who held the famous bike race!"

"Isn't that going a little far?" asked Dawn dubiously.

"Not at all," said Terri as they started riding again. "No one has ever thought of such a brilliant idea."

"Well, I don't know about that, but we're the first with this idea, so it could be famous," said Linda.

"Maybe we can get a write-up in the paper," suggested Angela. "It's a 'high-visibility' idea. We haven't done anything really spectacular since—"

"Since Dawn won one hundred thousand dollars," supplied Linda.

"Or since Terri gave Tommy a black eye," said Sonya, giggling.

Terri frowned. "That wasn't exactly front-page news."

Some time before the girls had formed a "High-Visibility Club" for the purpose of getting themselves noticed around school.

When they arrived at school they were all talking at once. "If it's a big enough event, we could maybe get it on the local news channel," said Terri. "My mom has connections."

"Oh, goody!" cried Dawn as they entered the school building.

The bell rang, and all the girls took off for class. On the way Linda said, "Let's meet at my house after school to discuss this." She loved it when they came up with wonderful ideas and schemes. And she knew this was one of the best ideas yet!

After school the girls rode as quickly as they could to Linda's house. Monique would come over later by car.

When they walked in they found Jennifer watching TV. She smiled happily when she saw Linda, but her expression changed when she noticed the other girls.

"I didn't know you were bringing *them* home with you," she whispered to Linda.

"We have this great idea!" Linda said, ignoring Jennifer's remark. She quickly told Jennifer all about the bike race.

Jennifer frowned. "I don't like riding bikes."

"What?" Linda couldn't believe her ears. Then she remembered how nervous Jennifer had been about riding in the street on Sunday. Jennifer used to love riding bikes, Linda thought.

"You just want to sit around and talk about your famous father," said Terri.

"I do not!" retorted Jennifer.

"That's not fair, Terri," said Linda. "Jennifer is a good bike rider."

"Well, she doesn't sound like it," said Terri, glaring at Jennifer.

"Come on. Let's not fight," said Dawn worriedly. She was always the first to put a stop to fights. "I think we should have our meeting now."

"Okay. Any suggestions, Jennifer?" asked Sonya.

"I think you should have a show with juggling acts and fire eaters," said Jennifer.

"But we already decided to have a bike race," said Terri.

Jennifer stared back at her in stony silence.

Linda went into the kitchen to get some snacks, hoping food would make everyone feel better. The first thing she noticed when she opened the refrigerator was a big angel food cake wearing a sign that said "Hands Off."

There wasn't much to snack on, but she finally settled on some apples, which she brought upstairs.

In her room everyone but Jennifer was talking excitedly. Jennifer was sitting primly on her bed, not saying a word. While the girls continued their plans she picked up three of the apples and began to juggle them.

"Hey, that's good," said Angela. "How do you do that?"

"Easy, like this," said Jennifer, demonstrating. Everyone stopped talking to watch her.

"Will everyone please pay attention to business?" asked Linda, finally tired of Jennifer and her trick.

"If we're going to make any money from this, we have to charge an entry fee," said Dawn. "How much shall we charge?"

"A dollar a bike?" suggested Sonya.

"I think we should have different kinds of races and offer prizes," said Sonya.

"We could have a decorated-bike contest, a slowest race, and a fastest race," said Angela.

"We can have races for different ages, too," said Terri.

"Oh, and a funniest-bike contest!" added Dawn, jumping up in excitement.

"We have to advertise—all over town," said Terri thoughtfully.

"Which means tons of posters," Linda said.

"A massive advertising campaign," said Sonya.

While they were talking Jennifer slipped out of the room and went downstairs. Soon the girls hopped on their bikes to ride home.

A few minutes later Mrs. Carmichael pulled up in the driveway. A short two minutes after that she was shouting, "Linda! Come down here this instant!"

Linda and Jennifer were sitting in Linda's bedroom.

"Uh-oh. She must know about the shoes," said Linda.

Jennifer shrugged. "Maybe not."

Linda skipped down the stairs, thinking wildly. What would she say to her mom? How could she explain what had happened without telling on Jennifer?

Mrs. Carmichael was in the kitchen, holding her angel food cake. "Did you eat this cake?" she asked, her eyes dark and angry.

Linda gazed at the cake, which was missing a single large slice. "No, Mom. You had a sign on it." She was so relieved! It had nothing to do with the shoes!

"That's right. So who ate it?" demanded Mrs. Carmichael.

"Maybe Jon," suggested Linda.

"He's not home. I made this cake to take to work tomorrow for an office party. You all know better than to eat something that's labeled," said Mrs. Carmichael. Linda knew how important her mother's new part-time job and social life were to her.

"Look, Mom. I didn't eat it, okay? Maybe the note got knocked off the cake, and then someone came along and ate it without knowing what it was for," Linda said quickly.

"Possibly. The sign was lying at the bottom of the refrigerator," Mrs. Carmichael said thoughtfully. "At any rate, I'll have to buy a cake now, because I don't have time tonight to make one."

"I'm sorry," Linda said. "I'll get it for you." She felt so bad about the cake, the shoes—just everything. It made her feel a little sick.

"Let's go together," suggested her mother. "We'll take Jennifer, too. I'm sure she'd love to see our fabulous Fresh Bakery."

While Mrs. Carmichael dialed the Fresh Bakery, Linda went upstairs to get Jennifer.

"I guess you heard the whole thing," Linda said as she pulled on a sweater. "Did you eat that cake?"

"Well, yes, but I didn't know what it was for," she replied. "You won't tell on me, will you, Linda?"

Linda's stomach seemed to twist into a knot at Jennifer's words. "Jennifer, that cake was for my mom's office party! Can't you read? The sign said 'Hands Off!' "

"Well, excuse me," said Jennifer huffily. "There was no sign on it when I looked in the refrigerator. I thought I was supposed to make myself at home."

"Explain that to my mom, please," said Linda.

"No!"

"Jennifer, I think you should be honest with my mom. She'll understand."

"I can't do that!" cried Jennifer, her eyes filling with quick tears.

"Why not?" demanded Linda. "She's not a monster."

"It's too embarrassing," Jennifer insisted. Linda handed her a tissue. "She'll think I'm awful."

"No, she won't. My mom is the most understanding mom in the world," said Linda. She knew she was right. Her mother was really easygoing. "She doesn't think anybody's awful. And she doesn't judge people unfairly."

"Girls!" called Mrs. Carmichael.

Linda started for the door, but Jennifer laid a hand on her arm. "Please don't say anything!" she pleaded.

"I'm not going to. It's up to you to come clean, Jen. Not me. But if you don't, I may not speak to you ever again," Linda told her. Then she turned and walked quickly downstairs.

During the drive to the Fresh Bakery, Linda listened to Jennifer make conversation. Her voice sounded much higher than usual.

"We have a bakery that delivers to our house," Jennifer was saying. "It's not even this far away." She sounded like a phony actress, Linda decided.

At the bakery Linda got out of the car first and went inside to greet the Selbys. Mr. and Mrs. Selby were in the bakery storefront, helping a customer.

"Well, look who's here!" cried Mr. Selby. He strode around the counter to give Linda a big hug.

"Meet my friend from Los Angeles, Jennifer," said Linda.

Shyly, Jennifer came forward and shook Mr. and Mrs. Selby's hands.

"Nice to meet a friend of Linda's. Dawn told me all about you," said Mrs. Selby. Her light blond hair was cut short around a small, beaming face.

"You and Dawn look alike," said Jennifer.

She laughed. "Yes. People say we should do mother-and-daughter commercials."

Mrs. Carmichael hugged the Selbys, too. Then Mr. Selby went into the back and came out carrying a huge angel food cake.

"What do you think of this one?" he asked proudly.

Linda loved how the Selbys were so proud of their bakery goods.

"It looks so good, we'll have to build a cage around it to keep people away," said Mrs. Carmichael, laughing.

"One person in particular," Linda muttered under breath. She glared at Jennifer, and Jennifer glared back.

"What a good idea! We could build cake cages," Mr. Selby exclaimed.

Mrs. Carmichael carried the boxed cake carefully to the car, while the girls said goodbye to the Selbys.

"I'm taking the cake straight to the office so I don't have to worry about it," she said.

Linda and Jennifer waited in the car while Mrs. Carmichael took the cake into her office, along with a new sign.

"The Selbys really helped my family when we first moved to town," explained Linda, while her mom was gone. "They gave Jon a job, and Dawn helped me when I got into trouble for stealing. This is the first place we've lived long enough to have lots of friends."

"As long as you have one friend, you're okay," said Jennifer. She picked at a thread on her jean jacket.

"But having a group of friends is extra nice," Linda explained. "I feel really lucky having Angela, Terri, Sonya, Dawn, and now Monique. Did you know that some places I've lived I didn't make one single friend?"

Jennifer gazed at her. "No, I didn't know that. But if you ask me, I don't think your friends are all that great."

Linda opened her mouth in shock. "How can you say that?"

"Well, Sonya's stuck on herself. Terri's a bigmouth. Angela is too dramatic. Dawn is a wimp. And Monique is so sickly," Jennifer answered, ticking the girls off on her fingers.

"My friends aren't like that at all!" shouted Linda. She wanted to cry. She wanted to jump out of the car and run as far away from Jennifer as she could get. "Anyway, I wouldn't talk if I were you. You're a prissy snob."

"I am not. What makes you think you're so perfect?" said Jennifer.

"I don't think I am," insisted Linda. "You know you won't even give my friends a chance. You don't even know them yet."

Jennifer shrugged and stared out the window.

Linda wasn't sure if she wanted to give Jennifer any more chances. She couldn't bear to hear anyone say anything bad about her best friends!

Chapter Six

ஃ

After school Wednesday Linda went home to collect Jennifer to bring her to Angela's. They were going to make posters for the bike race on Saturday.

The two girls raced over to Angela's on their bikes, using a back road. Jennifer pulled a set of juggling squares out of her pocket and juggled while riding. They laughed as Linda charged through a mud puddle and sprayed mud up over both of them. Jennifer didn't even get upset about the fact that she had mud specks all over her windbreaker. As they walked up the path to Angela's apartment building Jennifer became quiet and sullen again. After what Jennifer had said about the girls, Linda hoped her friend wouldn't say or do anything awful that day.

When they arrived Terri, Angela, Monique, Dawn, and Sonya were already sitting on the carpet in Angela's room. Bits of construction paper, cut-up magazines, poster board, and felt pens were strewn across the floor.

"Hey, guys! Look what we came up with!" cried Sonya, holding up a round poster. It was designed like a bicycle

wheel. The poster read: "Come one, come all, to the fantabulous Gladstone Bike Race and Contest held on Saturday—"

"Oh, I love that!" cried Linda, plopping down next to her
friend.

"Is there such a word as *fantabulous?*" asked Jennifer dubiously.

Sonya flung her hands in the air. "Not really. I just love
making up words."

"Naming it the Gladstone Bike Race and Contest makes it
sound so official," said Terri.

"What day, what time, and where is it going to be held?"
asked Dawn.

"Good questions," said Terri. "Saturday's the best day."

"How about one in the afternoon?" suggested Angela.

"The perfect place would be a cul-de-sac," said Linda.
"Then we wouldn't have to worry about traffic."

"Your house is on a cul-de-sac," cried Monique.

"But the one a block over is better. The street is longer,"
said Linda.

"Mott Street," said Terri, swiftly filling in the blanks on
her poster. "Okay, fine. This Saturday, at one P.M."

"Yeah!" everyone yelled except Jennifer.

Everyone except Jennifer grabbed a felt pen or scissors and
started working.

"Come on, Jennifer. It'll be fun for you, too," urged Monique.

"I can't think of anything to draw," she said.

"Sure you can," said Linda. "Jennifer has always been a
good artist," she told the others.

"We're having a tricycle race, a funniest-bike race, a
slowest race, team races, and a couple of other events," said
Sonya. "There are millions of things you can draw."

Reluctantly, Jennifer picked up a black felt pen and began tracing the outline of a wheel, which she filled in with spokes.

"Oh, I almost forgot!" cried Dawn. "I bought this button-making kit." She tugged a box out of her backpack. The box opened, and blank buttons spilled across the carpet and everyone's legs.

"Oh, great, Dawn!" giggled Angela. "The great button blast."

"Hey, I've got an idea!" exclaimed Linda. "Let's make the buttons look like bike wheels, too. Like this." She demonstrated by drawing a wheel with spokes, then writing in "Gladstone Bike Race and Contest" across it.

"Oooh, that looks cute," said Dawn.

"We can hand these out at school," said Terri. "Everyone loves buttons."

"Let's take a whole bunch of buttons and posters to the bike store," suggested Monique.

"Super idea," said Terri. "You know, we do have to check this out with the town police, but they'll probably block off the street for us."

"Good idea," all the girls, except Jennifer, answered.

Once all the posters and buttons were finished the girls rolled up the posters. Then they stuck them in their backpacks and rode downtown to distribute them and stop in at the police station.

Linda noticed how Jennifer lagged behind the others and was extra careful crossing streets. Why was she so scared? she wondered.

They stopped at Johnny's Bike Shop first. Linda marched in ahead of the others.

"Excuse me!" she asked the boy behind the counter. "We'd like to hang up some posters."

He turned around to face her. When he saw her, his face lit up with a big grin.

"Zack?" she stammered, her mouth dropping open.

"Yep. That's me," Zack said, smiling. "My uncle owns this store, and I came in to keep him company. He had to go to the bank for a minute and left me in charge. You're Linda, right?"

Her friends giggled. Linda felt her face grow hot. She suddenly remembered she was still wearing his and her medals under her shirt. "Yes, that's right."

"I never forget a face with a name," said Zack.

Not thinking, she backed up into a row of bicycles and knocked them over.

"Hey, easy!" cried Zack, moving out from behind the counter.

"Sorry," Linda said. She put down her backpack to help him pick up the bikes. "I didn't mean to do that."

"It's okay."

She picked up a handful of the posters. The two medals flopped out of her shirt, but she clutched the posters against her chest.

"Careful, you're going to squash the posters," warned Terri, who was now standing next to her.

Zack looked down at the rolled-up posters. "So you want to hang up a few posters?"

"Uh, y-yes," stammered Linda.

"Maybe you'd like to have a few buttons up here at the counter for your customers," said Terri. She produced a box of the handmade buttons and took out a couple to show Zack.

"Nice buttons. Sounds like a fun bike race," he said.

Linda unrolled one of the round posters.

"Hey, very catchy." He walked around with one, trying it

out on different walls. Then, finally, he put it inside the front door.

"Oh, good! People will see it the minute they open the door!" cried Dawn.

"Then we'll put another one by the counter," said Zack. "I know my uncle likes to promote bike races." He got out some thumbtacks and put up another poster.

Linda was standing right next to Zack, watching his every move. She had lowered the rest of the posters to her side, so he saw her medals.

"You're still wearing the medals. Do you take them off to take a bath?" he teased.

"Of course I do. I just wear them for good luck," she explained, blushing.

Suddenly Jennifer appeared at her other side.

"Linda, I found out there's a bead store downtown somewhere. I really need to go there," she said.

"Now?" asked Linda, making a face at her.

"Well, yes. Will you take me there?" asked Jennifer.

The friends exchanged glances. Linda felt ready to explode.

Zack finished with the poster and smiled at Linda. "Well, if you have to leave, I'll say goodbye, then."

"Goodbye, Zack," said Linda, forcing a smile.

"See you at the bike race!" he called as the girls trudged out the door.

Once they were safely out of hearing range Sonya almost shouted, "Yeow! Did you hear that?"

"He'll see you at the bike race, Linda," whispered Angela dreamily.

Linda glared at her. "Yes, I heard. No thanks to you, Jen."

"I didn't do anything!" Jennifer insisted.

"Stop fighting!" cried Dawn.

"That has to be the most romantic thing that has happened lately," exclaimed Angela, clutching her heart.

Terri shook her head. "The best part is that we now have an important contact at the bike store."

"Uh-oh. Don't look now," warned Sonya, staring across the street.

Celia and Polly were walking across the street toward the girls. Celia smiled at them all.

"What's the excitement all about?" she asked sweetly.

"We're having a bike race," said Dawn. Then she unrolled a poster for Celia to look at. "See?"

Terri pushed the poster right in front of Celia's eyes.

"Yes, I see," she said, pushing the poster away. "It looks like baby stuff to me."

Terri planted her hands on her hips. "It's going to be very sophisticated."

"With all kinds of races," added Monique.

"Here. Have a button," offered Linda. She stepped forward and tried to pin the button right on Celia's chest.

Linda accidentally stuck her with the pin. Celia flinched. "Ouch! Get away from me!" The button clattered to the pavement.

"Sorry. Just wanted to put it where it would be noticed," Linda said, smiling. "Want one, Polly?"

Polly backed away. "Uh, no thanks. I'll pass."

Angela, Terri, and Sonya burst out laughing. Celia turned, grabbing Polly by the sleeve so that she almost fell over. The two girls stomped off.

"Can't you just see Celia wearing a button on each of her you-know-whats?" said Angela, giggling.

"Those you-know-whats are commonly known as breasts, Angie," corrected Terri.

Everyone giggled.

Once Celia and Polly were safely out of sight Linda turned to Jennifer. "I'd like to know what's the big deal with the bead store."

Jennifer frowned. "I just wanted to get some beads, Lin."

"Yes, but you never mentioned it until the very second I was standing there talking with Zack," said Linda suspiciously. "It makes me think you really didn't want me to talk to him."

"That's not true. I just thought of it while we were in the store," replied Jennifer.

"You just had a sudden, desperate need for beads," sang Angela. "I get those for Twinkies."

"What a bead brain!" quipped Sonya.

Since her friends were treating this lightly, Linda decided to let it go. Also, she didn't want to tell Jennifer off in front of her friends, but she really wanted to.

"Okay, let's go to the bead store," she said. As she jumped on her bike she still wondered why Jennifer had made such a point of going to the bead store while she was talking to Zack.

Chapter Seven

On Thursday after school Jennifer was waiting at the bike racks for Linda. Two pairs of roller skates hung over her handlebars.

By the time Linda reached the area, Jennifer had climbed onto the bike rack and was walking along it as if it were a tightrope. Boys came out and clustered around her. Howard was in the front row carrying his Gladstone Gopher costume.

"Jen, you'd better get down from there before Ms. Prince, the principal, comes out and sees you," Linda warned.

"What can she do to me?" she asked. "I don't go to this school."

"Well, get down before you get killed, then," said Linda.

"Watch me." Jennifer then proceeded to jump from the rack over the bikes in a single bound. She landed flat on her hands and knees. "Ouch." Her audience laughed and applauded.

"You're not Superwoman," said Linda, picking up her friend. "But you're awfully brave."

Dawn, Terri, Sonya, Angela, and Monique came up behind Linda.

"That was some jump," said Terri admiringly.

"Thanks." Jennifer turned to Linda. "I thought you might like to go roller skating."

"Oooh! Roller skating sounds like fun!" cried Dawn.

"Well, thanks for asking, but I've got a gopher commitment after school," said Howard, making snorty gopher noises.

Sonya jabbed him in the ribs with her elbow. "Not you, silly. She's asking us." She became jealous when Howard showed any interest in other girls.

Jennifer turned bright red. "Well, actually, I was asking Linda," she said in a soft voice.

"Oh," Terri said, rolling her eyes.

"I guess that means we're out," said Angela mournfully.

Dawn's expression fell. "We can go by ourselves," she said, looking at Angela.

"Linda and I have been planning this for a long time," said Jennifer.

"We have?" asked Linda.

"Did you reserve all the sidewalks for this afternoon?" asked Terri jokingly.

Linda nudged Terri. "It doesn't have anything to do with you guys. Jennifer and I just need to spend some time together," she said.

"I understand," said Dawn.

"Why don't we all meet at Sundaze in the mall later?" suggested Linda.

"Okay. Five o'clock," said Terri. "We need to buy prizes for the race, anyway."

They said goodbye. Linda got on her bike. "I have to take my backpack home first. Then we can skate."

"I'm glad you told your friends that we needed to spend

some time together," said Jennifer happily. "It seems like we have to do everything with them."

"They're a lot of fun," replied Linda, feeling defensive. She couldn't tell Jennifer that she wished she was with her other friends instead of with her. "It wasn't very nice of you to act like that in front of them."

Jennifer ignored her. "Come on, let's hurry up. I've been waiting all day for you to get out of school so that we could skate."

Linda felt a little torn as she coasted down the hill in front of Jennifer. Jennifer had been nice to her since last night after the incident with Zack. She had helped Linda with all her chores.

After they got home and put their bikes away, the two girls sat on the curb to lace up their skates.

They skated through the park and down a side street with their shoes hanging off their shoulders.

"You know, I think you really should try to get to know my friends, Jennifer," said Linda.

"I'm not going to be here that long," Jennifer told her. "Besides, I came to Gladstone to visit you, not them."

"I know, but we could have so much fun together if—" She stopped herself.

"If what?" demanded Jennifer, her eyes narrowing. "If I wasn't around?"

"No, I didn't mean that," Linda replied quickly. "I want you here, but I want you to like my friends, too. Why don't you ever want to hang around them?"

Jennifer, who had been skating in the street, made a flying jump up over the curb onto the sidewalk. She spun and turned around in midair. Linda's stomach flipped as she watched.

Then Jennifer did a back flip and landed right in front of Linda. They were just outside a department store.

"Because I don't like to hang out with groups of kids. I don't like organized activities. My whole life is organized for me, Lin," she explained. "I just wanted to spend time with you."

"Well, my friends are a big part of my life, and I don't like cutting them out," said Linda. "I think you were really mean to them, not asking them to go skating with us."

"They understood. Anyway, you're supposed to do what I want because I'm visiting you," Jennifer said.

"Oh, yeah?" Linda glared at her.

"Yeah." Jennifer glared back fiercely.

"Jennifer, sometimes you can be a real jerk," said Linda, her skate rolling out from under her.

She lost her balance and frantically reached for Jennifer, making her lose her balance, too. Jennifer's legs went in opposite directions until she was almost in a perfect split, Linda clinging to her neck with a death grip.

Finally both girls sat down hard on the pavement, Linda on top of Jennifer. They just lay there, laughing. People entering the department store stopped to stare and ask if they could help.

"Thanks. I think we're okay," Jennifer said between giggles.

"I'm glad we're wearing jeans!" spluttered Linda, trying to stand up.

"What were you saying about me being a jerk?" asked Jennifer, grinning down at her friend.

The shadow of a person fell across Linda at that moment. She turned and looked up at Celia Forester.

"I've seen you look pretty stupid, but this is the stupidest," said Celia, laughing.

Linda glared at her. "I'd close my mouth right now if I were you, because something big and ugly is about to fly in it."

Celia clamped her mouth shut and stared down at Linda.

Linda laughed as she stood up.

"We had an accident," explained Jennifer. "That was why we were sprawled out on the sidewalk."

"Do they do this in Hollywood?" Celia asked Jennifer.

"Only in acting classes," said Jennifer.

"You take acting classes down there?" Celia inquired. She was really interested now.

"Well, sure. I take class from the same person that Biff Nightingale takes from," said Jennifer, making a graceful turn on her skates.

"Wow. I'd just love to go to Hollywood and act. I think I could be a real actress someday," Celia said, twirling around on the sidewalk. Her long red hair fanned out behind her.

"Well, I guess you could," replied Jennifer. "You're pretty enough."

"Oh, you think so?" Celia sighed dramatically. "But I happen to be talented, too."

"Well, if they have any roles for royal pains, you should get the part," said Linda, giggling.

"Ha-ha-ha, Carmichael," said Celia. "I've been in several school productions. I was Maria in *West Side Story*. Did Linda tell you that?"

"No, she didn't mention it," answered Jennifer.

Linda tapped Jennifer on the shoulder. "Uh, sorry to interrupt, but we have to be somewhere at five."

"Okay. Well, 'bye, Celia. See you around," said Jennifer, waving.

Celia fluttered her fingers in a wave. " 'Bye, dahling."

Linda and Jennifer started skating again.

"You have to be careful with her," warned Linda. "She's the snobbiest, meanest girl in our sixth grade class."

"She seems nice," said Jennifer.

"Nice?" said Linda, not believing her ears. Suddenly she swerved to avoid hitting a pedestrian. "Attila the Hun was nice compared to Celia. Celia is only nice if she wants something from you."

"What could she want from me?" asked Jennifer. "She doesn't even *know* me!"

"She wants to know you because you live in L.A.," explained Linda. "She thinks you might be able to help her get into the movies."

"I still think she's nice," insisted Jennifer as they skated to the mall.

When they got there Jennifer skated straight through the open doors and around the inside fountain. Panicked, Linda followed her.

"Jen! Wait! We'll get in trouble for this!" she cried.

Jennifer was far ahead of her, laughing like crazy. Finally a security guard stopped her right outside Sundaze. Linda skated up beside her friend.

"Ladies, skating is not allowed in the mall," he told them sternly. "Take those skates off this instant."

"Aw, too bad," said Jennifer, grinning at Linda.

Inside Sundaze the other girls were already perched on pink- and white-striped stools, their faces half-hidden in menus. Like everybody else in the mall, they had looked up when they heard Linda and Jennifer being scolded by the security guard.

"Nice try," said Angela. "Now that you've got everyone's attention, what do you do for an encore?"

Jennifer flung her skates down on the floor, then jumped onto one of the pink-and-white stools and twirled around dangerously fast. "Wheee!"

"Jen, would you calm down, please?" asked Linda.

The waitress came over and gave Jennifer a stern look. "Young lady, if you can't behave, I'll have to ask you to leave."

"Uh-oh," Dawn said, cringing.

Jennifer stopped spinning and grinned at the girls.

"Hurrah!" said Monique. "Now that we're all here, I can order. I'm having an unchocolate delight!"

"I'm ordering a chocolate monstrosity," said Dawn.

"I'll have the extreme ice-cream float," Terri said.

"Somebody split something with me," pleaded Angela. Sonya agreed to split a small sundae with her.

Jennifer turned to Linda. "Could we split a soda?" she asked. "I didn't bring any money."

"I'll treat," offered Linda. They decided to each have a small hot fudgomaniac sundae.

"Look what we just bought," Monique said. She dumped the contents of a big bag onto the counter. Rolls of ribbon and crepe paper and boxes of candy spilled out.

"We're making our own winners' ribbons," explained Dawn proudly.

Linda felt left out because she hadn't gone with them on the important shopping expedition.

"We just met Celia," announced Jennifer.

"That is not a cause for celebration," grumbled Terri.

"I'm going to try not to let it spoil my appetite," said Linda.

"She seemed nice," said Jennifer.

"Celia is a lot of things, but 'nice' isn't one of them," corrected Angela.

Dawn placed her hand on Jennifer's arm. "I like almost everybody, but even I don't really like Celia."

"That's right. Dawn has given Celia more chances than any of the rest of us have," agreed Sonya.

"Dawn likes to think everyone has some good in them," said Terri.

"Well, I really think everybody does," Dawn said. "Even Celia, but I still can't like her."

"She was friendly to me," Jennifer insisted. Her sundae came, and she daintily dipped a spoon in it.

Terri leaned over and tapped her fudgy spoon on Jennifer's hand. Jennifer made a face and drew her hand back. "Celia would be friendly to a rattlesnake if she thought it would get her somewhere."

"Yes, but the rattlesnake would have to have a precious jewel in its ear or something," said Angela, her eyes shining.

"Do snakes have ears?" asked Dawn suddenly.

"They have inner ears," Linda answered.

Terri rolled her eyes. "Whatever. Celia obviously thinks you're valuable to her."

"I'm just an ordinary person," said Jennifer.

"No, you're not," said Linda. "You're my friend." She put her arms around Jennifer and squeezed.

When Linda and Jennifer arrived at Linda's house, they found Mrs. Carmichael on her hands and knees peering under the couch and chairs for her new shoes.

"I left them right in the box in the closet. They hadn't even been unwrapped!" she cried. "Have either of you girls seen them?"

"No," Linda and Jennifer chorused. Linda looked at Jennifer and frowned. How could Jennifer lie about the shoes and cause her to have to lie about them, too?

"What did they look like, Mrs. Carmichael?" Jennifer asked sweetly.

"Gold satin heels," Mrs. Carmichael said. Her head was half under the couch. "Just beautiful. I wonder if my dear husband hid them from me."

"Why would he do that, Mom?" asked Linda.

"Because he didn't like them," she replied. "But I just know he wouldn't do that to me. He knows how much I liked them!"

"No, he wouldn't," Linda agreed. "We'll look upstairs. Won't we, Jennifer?"

"Sure."

Once they were halfway up the stairs Linda whispered, "Now look what's happened! My mom's blaming my dad!"

"But it's not my fault!" insisted Jennifer loudly.

"Shhh!" Linda pressed her finger over her mouth. "Whose idea was it to keep this quiet? Why didn't you just tell her?"

"I was scared, Linda. You know that," Jennifer said.

"I was scared, too. And I'm lying to cover up for you," said Linda. "I don't like it, and I don't like you right now."

Jennifer's eyes filled with tears. "Why don't you just tell on me, then?"

"Because I'm your friend, that's why," said Linda in a low voice. "And friends stick up for each other. And they take care of each other, too." She stuck her face right up close to

Jennifer's. "That's something you probably don't know anything about because you don't have any feelings!"

"That's not fair, Linda! I do, too!" Jennifer cried.

With that, Jennifer whirled around, stomped up the stairs to Linda's room, and slammed the door behind her.

The telephone rang. It was Jennifer's mother. Jennifer picked up the phone in the second-floor hall. Linda listened. She heard Jennifer's muffled sobs, and her saying, "But, Mom, I don't want to! Please don't make me!"

After Jennifer hung up the receiver she was still crying. Linda felt awful. How could she say Jennifer didn't have any feelings? Something was definitely upsetting her. Linda went over and wrapped an arm around her shoulders.

"Hey, listen, I'm really sorry for what I said. I didn't mean it."

"Yes, you did," Jennifer said between sobs.

Linda felt even worse. "Look, it's going to be okay. You don't have to cry," she said comfortingly.

They went into Linda's room and closed the door behind them. Linda handed Jennifer a tissue.

"You don't understand anything, Linda," said Jennifer between tears.

"Tell me," urged Linda. "We always used to tell each other everything!"

"I can't tell you! I can't tell anyone!" declared Jennifer, throwing herself on her bed and burying her face in her pillow.

Chapter Eight

☸

"Hey, Jen. Since it's the last day of school and not much is going on today, why don't you come with me? I asked, and the principal said it was okay," Linda suggested on Friday as she was getting ready. Because Jennifer was feeling so blue about something going on back home, Linda hoped to cheer her up. "We're having a party in homeroom."

Jennifer surveyed her through bleary eyes. "That might be fun," she said.

"Get dressed," said Linda. "You can wear anything of mine that you want." She knew how much Jennifer loved to wear new and different things.

"I'm a size smaller than you," reminded Jennifer. She yanked off her shortie pajamas.

"Here. This ought to fit you," said Linda, handing her a navy and powder-blue sweatshirt. "I've outgrown it, and it's my favorite thing. In fact, you can have it."

"I can?" exclaimed Jennifer, holding the sweatshirt up to her. "Oh, thanks, Lin!"

"You're welcome," replied Linda, making a quick check of her appearance in the mirror. "Oh, I've got gymnastics after school!'' Hastily, Linda threw her leotard and tights into her backpack.

By the time Jennifer was finally ready, Terri, Dawn, Sonya, and Angela were out in front, waiting.

Terri was fuming. ''Hey, don't rush or anything,'' she said sarcastically. ''We've only been out here for fifteen minutes.''

''Five minutes,'' corrected Dawn.

''Jennifer's coming,'' said Linda, getting on her bike.

Jennifer looked extremely worried as she stared at the girls on their bikes. ''I'll just meet you guys there,'' she said.

''Jennifer, are you okay?'' asked Linda.

''I'm fine,'' Jennifer said quickly, but she was trembling.

Linda gave Jennifer directions to the school. She didn't know what to think of her friend.

The five girls rode as fast as they could to Gladstone Elementary. The first bell had already rung, and kids were scurrying to classes, shrieking and laughing. Terri raced ahead of the other girls, so she arrived on time. Linda waited for Jennifer until after the second bell rang, but she didn't show up.

Ms. Bell was in a good mood, and her desk was piled high with various goodies.

She folded her hands in front of her and ordered the class to be quiet. ''I want you to hear what I have to say, because it will make you feel good,'' she said.

Everyone fell silent. ''I've enjoyed having you all in my class this year, and I'm sorry to see you go. You've all been good students. But I'm glad you're graduating and going into junior high. I would hate to hold anyone back.''

Giggles traveled throughout the room. Howard made funny pig noises.

''I may even miss Howard's entertaining animalistic

noises," said Ms. Bell with a smile. Howard made dramatic sobbing sounds, and everyone laughed.

"Okay, now go on to your next classes. School is dismissed today at noon. When you return to this room at eleven o'clock I'll hand out the report cards, and then you can have your party," Ms. Bell said. Everyone cheered.

When the bell rang, the class moved out into the hall and to the next class. Linda found Jennifer in the hall in front of the office.

She took her hand. "Come on. We don't want to miss out on all the fun," said Linda, dragging her along.

After each teacher had said his or her goodbyes everyone came back to Ms. Bell's room.

As promised, Ms. Bell handed a small manila report card envelope to each student.

People groaned or squealed according to what kinds of grades they received. Linda had received good grades, so she didn't have anything to complain about.

Dawn arranged several cupcakes on a desktop. Each cupcake had a letter written in icing on its top, so that the message read: "Bike Race, Come One, Come All." Linda and Sonya handed out bike race buttons. Terri showed everyone a small clipping from the local paper on the bike race.

"We're entering the team bike race," Linda told the class. "Someone else is going to judge that event."

"Let the competition begin. We're going to be a team, too," said Howard, pointing to his friends. "Bobby, Lyle, Eddie, Tommy, and me."

Bobby Bugrin was very excited about the race. "I'm bringing my unicycle for the funniest-bike race," he told Angela.

"I'm decorating my bike with horns and things I brought back from Africa," said Howard. Howard had visited Africa during the fifth grade. His artifacts were well-known around school.

Lyle Kraus stationed himself in front of the punch bowl and poured punch into small Dixie cups. He poured the cups so full that everyone had to bend over the table to slurp up the extra punch so they wouldn't spill.

When school was out kids jammed the halls, flinging their empty backpacks into the air.

"No more school, no more teachers, no more homework!" yelled Eddie Martin. His backpack landed on Linda's head.

"Hey, Eddie, watch it." Linda shook empty bubble-gum wrappers out of her long hair.

"Sorry, Linda. Hey, see you at the bike race!" he called, loping down the hall.

Jennifer sighed heavily as she watched Linda clear out her locker. "Lin, I don't think I want to go to your gymnastics class today."

"Oh, come on. It'll be fun—more fun than hanging around the house," urged Linda.

"I thought maybe you and I could do something together again," said Jennifer.

"I have to go to my class, Jen!" cried Linda. "I can't miss class just because you're here."

Jennifer's expression crumpled. "I guess I'm not that important." She began walking away.

"Jennifer!" cried Linda.

Celia stopped in the hall to listen to the argument. Linda suddenly felt self-conscious.

"What're you staring at?" she asked Celia.

Celia shrugged. "Nothing." Then she ran to catch up with Jennifer. The two girls began laughing together.

"Watch out—looks like Celia's next victim," said Terri, who was standing behind Linda.

"Do you think that maybe this time Celia could be trying to be nice?" Dawn said hopefully.

"Fat chance," replied Terri.

Throughout her gymnastics class, which Celia cut, Linda couldn't stop thinking about Jennifer. She remembered how upset Jennifer was the night before when her mom had called. Jennifer hadn't even clowned around at all that day. She hadn't wanted to ride to school with the gang. Linda was also disappointed that Jennifer felt she couldn't talk to her about her problems. They had shared everything in the past.

At the same time that Linda felt guilty, she was also angry. Jennifer's visit was upsetting her entire life. She executed a few quick, fierce backflips, earning the applause of her teacher.

"Very good, Linda. You're in great form today."

"Thank you," she replied. It was strange how when she was really angry she could sometimes do very well at gymnastics.

When class was over Linda changed quickly and said goodbye to Terri.

"I have to go," she said.

"You're not going with me for a soda?" Terri asked, surprised.

"No. Jennifer's been so upset lately, I need to see her to find out what's going on," Linda explained.

Terri frowned. "It seems like Jennifer wants you all to herself."

"But she doesn't know anyone except me," Linda said.

"And us," Terri added. "She could be friends with us. But she doesn't like us. She'd rather be friends with Celia."

"That's not true!" cried Linda.

Terri shrugged and started walking toward the door. "Yes, it is."

Linda stood watching her go. She had an awful, sinking feeling that Terri was right.

Chapter Nine

⚘

Linda got home before Jennifer. Jennifer and Celia probably went somewhere together, she decided. Jennifer wouldn't understand why Celia could cut class but Linda couldn't. She went into her room and noticed what a mess it was. "I'm going to surprise Mom and clean up my room," she said out loud.

She began by dumping the wastebasket into a large plastic bag, which she got from the garage. When the garbage landed upside down in the bag she noticed a letter with unfamiliar handwriting. Linda fished it out of the bag and read the ending. It was from Jennifer's mother.

Linda fingered the letter. She thought she really shouldn't read it, because it was personal. But if it helped her to know Jennifer better, why not?

Dear Jen,
    I'm sorry to upset you like this, but Daddy and I still have our problems, and we don't seem to be able to work them out by staying together. I know this makes you unhappy, but we are definitely filing for divorce now. We

did talk about this with you before, so I know it's not a surprise.

As I told you before, this means that I'm going to work full time. My company is transferring me to another town. We'll start a completely new life.

Just remember that whatever happens, your daddy and I love you very much and want the best for you.

Love,
Mom

As Linda finished the letter tears slid down her face onto the page. Poor Jennifer! No wonder she was so upset.

"What are you doing?"

Linda jumped up suddenly, dropping the letter on the floor. "Oh, Jen, I'm sorry, I—"

Jennifer swooped down and picked up the letter. "You have no right to read my mail!"

"I know, but I was starting to clean my room, and I found it in the wastebasket."

"That's no excuse."

"Look, you wouldn't tell me what was wrong, and I had to know!" cried Linda. "We've been friends such a long time—"

Jennifer's eyes filled with tears. "It doesn't feel like we're very close anymore."

"I know, but I want us to be," said Linda. "Look, I know how you feel. I've got the world's weirdest parents. I know what it's like to have to move all over the place."

Jennifer clutched the letter to her chest. "You don't know what this is like. Your weird family is still together, and mine is falling apart!"

Jennifer ran down the stairs and out of the house in tears.

Linda watched from her window as her friend shimmied up the rope to the tree house. When she went to the tree house Jennifer wouldn't speak to her or come down. Linda didn't know what to do.

"Hey, there's a garage sale across the street. Want to go?" Linda asked Jennifer at breakfast the next morning. It was Saturday, the day of the bike race. Linda and Jennifer hadn't spoken to each other since the night before.

Jennifer shrugged disinterestedly. "Not really."

"We'd better go before all the bargains are gone," said Mrs. Carmichael, pulling on an old sweater. "Come on."

Linda and her mother charged out of the house and across the street. Card tables were stacked with kitchen gadgets. Wooden boxes held car and bicycle parts. A rack of old clothing blocked the pathway. Underneath it was a large cardboard box.

"Oh, Linda, look!" cried Mrs. Carmichael. She lifted a pair of shoes out of the box.

Linda's heart jumped. Dangling from her mother's fingers were the gold satin shoes! Linda had thrown them in Mr. Marcus's garbage, figuring that he'd just toss them out.

"These look just like my old shoes," exclaimed Mrs. Carmichael, examining them carefully. "They're my size, too, but they're completely ruined!"

Mr. Marcus trudged over to take a look. "Ah. I found them in my garbage can," he said. "They smelled like fudge."

Mrs. Carmichael sniffed the shoes. She turned to Linda. "Are you *sure* you don't know anything about these shoes, Linda?"

Linda felt her face and ears grow very hot. She wished Mr.

Marcus could go away so that she could speak to her mother in private. But he just stood there, listening.

"Uh, well, I had an accident with your shoes," she began. "I spilled hot fudge on them."

"Why didn't you just tell me?" she demanded angrily.

Fortunately, Mr. Marcus walked away from the argument.

"Well, I was going to. First of all, I took them to the shoemaker and found out they couldn't be cleaned. Then I dropped them in Mr. Marcus's garbage," Linda went on. "I almost have enough money to get you a new pair, so I figured I wouldn't ever have to tell you what happened."

"But you just allowed me to go on looking for these shoes!" declared Mrs. Carmichael, "knowing all the time what had happened."

"I'm really sorry, Mom," Linda said, feeling awful.

"I'm surprised at you," Mrs. Carmichael said, shaking her head. "I thought you had learned to be honest, Linda."

"You can trust me, I p-promise," stammered Linda. She said nothing about Jennifer.

"How? You lied to me. Look, I need my shoes today," she said. "The wedding is tomorrow."

"I promise I'll get them for you," Linda said.

She ran home and upstairs to find Jennifer. Her friend was lying on her bed, reading a movie magazine. Suddenly the idea that Jennifer was reading about famous people bugged her.

"Jennifer, we have an emergency. My mom found her shoes," she announced, flopping onto her bed. "I told her I messed them up and that I planned to replace them."

Jennifer put down her magazine. "Geez, I'm sorry, Lin. Anything I can do to help?"

"Yes. The wedding is tomorrow at four. I need the money

for the shoes by today or early tomorrow afternoon when the mall opens. I don't know if we'll be able to make enough money at the bike race today,'' Linda went on. ''Do you think you could ask your mom to pay for the shoes?''

''No way. My mom would have a fit!'' cried Jennifer.

''But it's your fault. You messed them up, and you're acting like it's no big deal. You should work at the bike race to earn the money for the shoes. I thought of the idea so that we could get the shoes, but you've done nothing.''

''I helped make posters,'' Jennifer said.

''After I twisted your arm,'' Linda pointed out. ''You've been a royal pain, Jen. You always were kind of a whiner, but now you're a royal pain.''

''I was not always a whiner!'' she yelled. ''And *I'm* not a pain, *you're* a pain! A big, double-decker pain!'' Jennifer picked up her movie magazine and stomped out of the room.

Linda followed her and grabbed her by the arm. ''You know what, Jen? You're all wrapped up in your own problems so you don't care about anybody except yourself. You're not the friend I thought you were.''

Jennifer stood on tiptoe to look Linda straight in the eye. ''You know what, Lin? You're right. I don't care about anybody. I don't care if you get run over by a ten-ton truck!''

Linda watched Jennifer run down the stairs. She was so mad at her that she was glad she was gone. All Linda could think about was how she would get the shoes. The next day was Sunday. She still didn't want to tell her friends about the trouble she was in, and Jennifer was no help at all. Would she be able to earn enough money at the bike race for her mother's shoes?

* * *

No one could miss the Mott Street cul-de-sac with its crepe-paper streamers and bike race signs. The street was well known because it ended in a long flight of steps that went down into a deep, heavily wooded canyon.

Linda, Jennifer, and the other girls watched the first arrivals for the funniest-bike contest.

"Look at Bobby!" cried Angela. He wore a horrible, bloody mask with five eyes on its face. His unicycle was decorated with little plastic skulls, bones, and eyeballs.

Lyle Kraus was dressed as a chili pepper. His bike was decorated in red crepe paper with real dried red peppers hanging off it.

"Hey, Lyle. Your outfit is hot stuff!" cried Linda, waving at him.

"Don't say that. He'll get outrageous," warned Terri.

Tommy rode over to Terri, dressed in a black cape and carrying a long rope looped over his shoulder. The spokes and handlebars of his bike were woven with black and red crepe paper.

"Who are you supposed to be?" she asked.

"I'm a tightrope rider," he replied, grinning at her.

"That's the most original idea yet!" cried Dawn.

"Look who's coming, guys!" called Sonya, pointing at Howard.

Animal horns, shells, and tiny drums hung from his handlebars. His costume was a fake zebra skin sewn onto his T-shirt. He blew on the horns, clanked the shells like castanets, and beat the drums as he rode.

"You are wild, Howard," said Sonya,

Howard sighed. "That's the sweetest thing you've ever said to me."

A couple of little girls came dressed as robots with their

bikes covered in tin foil. One child had made her bike into a cardboard horse.

"Okay, everybody parade around in a circle," ordered Terri. "We'll judge the bikes now."

Dawn, Angela, Sonya, Monique, and Linda sat down on metal folding chairs and put their heads together. Jennifer sat next to them and pouted. Linda and Jennifer had not exchanged one word since their fight the previous day.

"I really like the horse," said Sonya. "But, of course, I love Howard's African idea."

"I like the tightrope rider," said Angela.

"I do, too, but I can't vote for him," said Terri, crossing her arms. "It wouldn't be fair."

"Come on, Terri. Just think of who's best, not which boy you're in love with," said Angela, giggling.

"I'm *not* in love with Tommy," she declared.

Tommy unlooped his rope and tried to ride his bike along it. Everyone giggled.

"The chili pepper is pretty cute," said Monique.

"Come on, let's vote!" Terri held out a sequined hat. Each of the girls put a secret ballot inside it.

Then Terri unfolded the papers in front of each of the contestants.

"The winners of the funniest-bike contest are: first place, Howard Tarter for his African bike and Tommy Atwood for his tightrope bike. Second place to the girls with the robot bikes—" A squeal arose from the little girls.

"And third place to Lyle for his chili-pepper bike. Fourth place goes to the horse bike."

Terri handed out small boxes of chocolates and blue ribbons for the first-place winners, and different colored ribbons for the other winners.

While everyone was cheering for the winners, Dawn got the contestants ready for the slowest-bike race.

Linda was tired of hanging around near Jennifer. It felt awful to be standing there, wanting to wring her neck. So she started walking. She noticed Celia approaching, all decked out in a bright red minidress with a long grosgrain ribbon in her hair. She stopped next to the bike rack where the best friends had their bikes. Because she didn't want to have to talk to Celia at that moment, Linda walked in the opposite direction.

A few minutes later Jennifer caught up with Linda. She was holding a small oil can.

"Lin, I'm sorry for what I said yesterday. Look, I found a way to help. This is supposed to make your bikes work perfectly," she said. "It's from the bike store."

Linda's heart skipped a beat. "Johnny's?" she asked.

"Yes. Come on." Jennifer led the way back to the bike rack.

Linda took the oil can from her and squirted the thick oil onto Dawn's chain. Dawn, Angela, Sonya, Terri, and Monique came over to claim their bikes.

"It smells funny," she said.

"It sure doesn't smell like perfume," said Jennifer.

"Dawn, try out your bike," said Linda.

Dawn leapt on her bike and rode a short distance. Suddenly her bike wheels locked up. The bike bucked and stopped, and Dawn fell over on her side.

"Ouch!" she cried, rubbing her ankle. She got up and hopped on one foot. "Something stopped my bike."

"Are you okay?" asked Sonya. The girls rushed over to see if she was all right.

"The bike just stopped," explained Dawn.

Linda examined Dawn's wheels, which seemed okay. Then she looked at the chain. The so-called oil had hardened on the chain, preventing the bike from moving! No wonder Dawn had fallen off.

A short distance away Celia and her friends were giggling about Dawn's accident.

"I'd like to see you fall on your face," Terri shouted angrily, clenching her fists.

"Don't start anything," warned Dawn.

Linda sniffed the oil can again. She rubbed a drop of the substance between her fingers to test its stick. "You know what this stuff is?"

"Oil?" guessed Dawn.

"No, it's an oozy glue that dries in about three minutes, like contact cement," said Linda. "And I put it on Dawn's chainwheel."

"Linda, why did you do that?" asked Terri. "Dawn could've been killed!"

"Do you think I did it on purpose?" exclaimed Linda. "I didn't know what was in the can!"

"You should've been more careful," said Terri huffily.

"I'm sure Linda didn't mean it," said Dawn.

"Yeah. She wouldn't do that on purpose," added Angela.

"The stuff came from Johnny's Bike Shop," Linda told them. "Wait a minute. Why are the clones over there laughing? Did they have anything to do with this?"

"Celia gave it to me. And she told me it came from Johnny's," said Jennifer, looking over at Celia. "She told me it would make the bikes go faster."

"That liar!" exclaimed Terri.

"Celia fooled you, Jennifer," said Linda. "It looks like Celia's up to her old tricks again."

"Maybe it was Jennifer's idea," suggested Terri, glaring at Jennifer.

"No, it wasn't!" cried Jennifer. "I was trying to be helpful!"

Linda was still smarting from their argument the day before. "Since when?" she asked, suddenly angry.

"Since I realized that I wasn't being very helpful," explained Jennifer.

"Well, you really blew it this time, Jen," said Linda, walking away. She wanted to get as far from Jennifer as she possibly could.

Chapter Ten

⊞

"Okay, everybody! Line up for the eleven-to-thirteen-year-old team bike race!" called Monique, waving two big red flags. She was in charge of the race, while Angela, Dawn, Terry, Linda, and Sonya made up one of the five-person teams.

"I can't ride my bike!" wailed Dawn. "I can't press down on the pedal with my ankle sore like this."

Linda and Angela came over to investigate. Linda pulled down Dawn's sock to get a look at her swollen ankle.

"It doesn't look good," said Linda. "I'll take you up to my house for some ice."

"No, wait!" exclaimed Dawn. "I want to see the race first."

"What're we going to do?" cried Angela. "We need a fifth rider now."

"The only person left is Jennifer," said Terri.

Linda helped Dawn over to someone's lawn so she could rest. Jennifer was right behind her.

"If it hadn't been for you, this would never have happened," Linda told Jennifer.

"You blame me right away," Jennifer cried. "I didn't know there was glue in that can!"

"Oh, and you didn't know you were ruining my mom's new shoes, either, did you?" Linda blurted out in anger.

"New shoes?" chorused the other girls, who had followed them.

Jennifer turned beet red and covered her face with her hands while Linda told the whole story of the shoes.

"Jennifer went into my mom's closet and took a pair of brand-new shoes that she planned to wear to a wedding tomorrow," Linda explained. "She dropped hot fudge sauce on them. We tried to get them cleaned, but they were completely ruined. I threw them in my neighbor's garbage can. So I came up with this idea of the bike race to make money for new shoes. I figured Jennifer would work on the race, since it's her fault the shoes are ruined. Yesterday my mom and I went to our neighbor's garage sale, and guess what? He had pulled the fudgy shoes out of the garbage and was selling them! She was furious. I had to tell her the whole story. Except I left out the part about who actually dropped the fudge sauce on the shoes."

All eyes turned to Jennifer.

"Linda forgot to mention that I made the hot fudge sundae for her as a treat," said Jennifer.

"So what? It sounds like you got her in a big mess!" exclaimed Angela.

"I covered up for Jen because she's my friend," Linda said. "But I feel like I've just been telling one little white lie after another."

"They don't sound little or white to me," said Monique.

"Linda, we can help you with the money," Dawn offered, patting her shoulder.

"Thanks, Dawn," Linda said, squeezing her friend warmly. She loved the way her friends came through for her when things were tough.

"I hate to break this up, but we've got a race to ride," said Terri, standing over Linda and Dawn.

Linda gazed at Jennifer. "Okay, what about this idea? Jen, you ride in the race in Dawn's place."

"I told you, I don't like riding bikes," Jennifer said, suddenly terrified. "I'll help in any other way."

"Oh, come on. We're desperate! We need you!" cried Sonya.

"Yeah. It's not fair. You'd have fun, and you don't have anything else to do," Angela pointed out.

"You're a good bike rider," said Linda. "You can ride with no hands, and juggle, and—"

"Hey, cool it guys!" ordered Terri. "I think she'll make us lose with that creepy attitude of hers."

"Oh, yeah. I changed my mind. I don't want her to ride with us," said Sonya.

"You have to have your heart in it, Jennifer, or else it isn't going to work," said Dawn.

"I agree. Maybe one of the boys will ride for us," suggested Angela. She gazed over at the boys, who were busy throwing crepe-paper spitballs at one another.

Jennifer bit her lip, and her face turned bright red. She looked like she was trying hard not to cry in front of everyone. "Well, that's just fine with me," she shouted. Then she whirled around and ran down the log steps that led into the canyon.

"She's probably just faking crying," said Angela.

"Yeah, she's really been a lousy friend to you, Linda," said Sonya loyally.

"Good friends don't get each other in trouble like that," said Dawn. "I wonder why she ran into the canyon."

"She just wants Linda to go running after her," said Terri. "I'm glad she's gone."

Linda gasped. Suddenly her anger at Jennifer seemed unimportant. "Terri, Jennifer doesn't know where she's going! She could get lost!"

"Or eaten by a bear," added Angela, smirking.

"Don't be mean, you guys! Jennifer's really unhappy. And you know how nutty she is. Why, she might just stay down there all night!" cried Linda. With tears filling her eyes she took off down the log steps Jennifer had taken into the canyon.

The canyon was heavily wooded. The steps led down to a narrow path that ran along the edge of the canyon. A sheer drop fell off on one side. Linda thought about how Jennifer liked dangerous things like tightrope walking or jumping off a high dive. What if she fell off the path?

Brushing the unpleasant thought aside, Linda ran nimbly down the little trail to where it forked into four trails. Which way would Jennifer have taken? she wondered.

"I could be here all night," she grumbled to herself. One trail was very skinny and overgrown with poison oak, so she probably wouldn't go on that one. The next led to an open park cabin, but Jennifer wouldn't know that. The other two led directly to the floor of the canyon.

On a hunch Linda decided to take the trail that led to the cabin. It was rocky and treacherous, just the kind of trail that would appeal to Jennifer. As she approached the cabin she heard sobbing sounds coming from inside. She crouched down. Jennifer had to be inside.

Linda tiptoed over to the window and peered inside. Jennifer's head was buried in her hands.

Linda hopped gracefully up to the door in front of Jennifer. "Surprise."

Jennifer looked up and gasped. She started to smile. "Oh, Linda!"

"I thought I might find you here," Linda said.

"I was hoping you would just leave me in the woods forever," said Jennifer mournfully. She was sitting on a bench.

Linda sat down next to her. "Well, I thought about it. That way you couldn't ruin our bike race for us. But then I thought about you all alone down here, and I had to find you."

"It doesn't seem like we have anything in common anymore, Lin," said Jennifer. "I mean, you've got your other friends and everything."

"Yeah, I know it seems that way, but I still need you," insisted Linda. "Why don't you tell me everything that's been bugging you?"

"You'll make fun of me," Jennifer said, a big tear falling down her cheek.

"No, I won't. When have I made fun of you before? I've stuck up for you, even when I shouldn't have," Linda told her gently.

"Okay. It's just that you're so close to your other friends, and they don't like me," she mumbled.

"They *would* like you, but they think you don't like *them*," said Linda. "They think you're stuck up."

"Me?"

"Yes. Because you talk about movie stars and your maid all the time, and you don't want to do anything we want to do," Linda explained. "You've always got some excuse not to do what we're doing, and you keep letting us down."

Jennifer burst into tears. "I do not! I'm not like that. You just don't understand!"

Linda handed her a tissue.

Jennifer blew her nose loudly, then started to talk. "I'm really jealous of you having all those good friends, I guess. I wanted it to be the way it used to be. Just you and me. Things just haven't been that great for me. I don't have a special friend at home right now."

"What about Mary Cavanaugh?"

"Oh, she's okay, but we're not as close as all that," said Jennifer miserably. "I just hate my life. My parents are getting a divorce—a divorce! They wanted me to go away for a couple of weeks while they decided what to do with their lives. Because of them, I don't even know where I'm going to live next year. My mom is supposed to get a job transfer, but we don't know where. It could be as far away as Boston. And my mom and dad don't know which of them I should live with, or where. They're both so busy, I never see them. They don't have time for me."

"Can't you ask to live with your dad in L.A.? I mean, he's such a big shot," said Linda.

Jennifer shook her head. "Listen, Linda. I made all that up about my dad. I wanted everyone to think I was exciting. He's not a screenwriter, and we don't have dinner with stars. He made a lot of money in stocks and then lost it all this year. Now he just works at a regular audio job for the studios. Sometimes he goes on location with a film, but famous people don't know who he is."

Linda patted her arm. "Well, you really impressed Celia, but it's no big deal. You don't have to have a famous father to impress me or my friends. Remember, we were friends when your dad was selling fake stocks and my dad was getting bailed out of jail. My friends know about my weird past and like me just the same.''

''Well, nobody except you knows about mine,'' said Jennifer. ''And besides, right now I don't want anyone to know about me. It's too embarrassing. I don't know where I fit in. I keep doing crazy things that get me in trouble, like what I did to your mom's shoes and the cake. I really don't mean to.''

''All you had to do was apologize,'' Linda pointed out.

''I was afraid your mother would think I was a bad influence on you and send me home,'' said Jennifer.

''She wouldn't,'' protested Linda.

''My mother would be really upset,'' Jennifer continued. ''I gave her lots to worry about this year—especially after my bike accident.''

''Bike accident?'' Linda asked with curiosity.

''Yes. A few months ago I was riding my bike along the side of a busy street. A car made a sharp right turn and hit me. I was in the hospital for a week.''

''Wow, Jen, I'm really sorry,'' said Linda. ''Why didn't you tell me?''

She shrugged. ''I don't like to talk about it. I've hated to ride bikes ever since.''

''Now I understand why you were so scared to ride,'' Linda said. Then she got an idea. ''Look, you know that saying— when you fall off a horse, you should get right back on it. Well, you can do the same thing with your bike.''

''This is different,'' Jennifer said dubiously.

''Not very different,'' Linda said. ''Look, you're braver than almost anybody I know. If you can do tightrope walking, there's no reason you can't ride a bike.'' She felt that Jennifer should try to make things better for herself.

"I have an idea—that is, if you want to prove you're a true friend and change everybody's opinion of you. Plus, I think you'll make yourself feel better."

"What?" Jennifer raised her tearstained face to gaze at her friend.

"Ride in this race."

Jennifer's eyes grew round and terrified. "I can't!"

Linda clasped her hand and squeezed it determinedly. "Come on, Jen. There's nothing to be afraid of. You can do it. It's the only way."

Chapter Eleven

As Linda and Jennifer approached the girls, Terri was standing in front of the others, arms crossed over her chest.

"It's about time," she said.

Linda nudged Jennifer in the ribs. "Jennifer has something to tell you."

"I do?" Jennifer asked in a squeaky voice. Linda nudged her again, harder. "I do." She cleared her throat. "I'd love to ride in your race."

"You would?" chorused the girls in surprise.

"Yes. And I'll do my best to win. And I'm really sorry for how I acted toward you guys," she said.

"How do we know you're not going to act up again?" asked Terri.

"Yeah. You still might make us lose. You are friendly with Celia," Sonya said suspiciously.

"Look, I don't have an excuse for how I acted, okay? I'm just having some problems right now," explained Jennifer. "My parents are getting a divorce and are moving away from each other. I don't know where I'm going to be living or going to school in the fall. I hardly ever see my parents anyway."

"Why?" asked Dawn.

"They're really busy and always traveling," she said. "I just wish that once they'd take me with them on a trip."

Terri remained unconvinced. "How can you be tough enough to do balancing acts but not want to ride in our race?"

Jennifer took a deep breath, then related the whole story of her bike accident.

"Oh, Jennifer, that's awful!" exclaimed Monique sympathetically.

Linda linked arms with Jennifer. "This is a chance for Jennifer to get back on a bike and stop being afraid."

"I really do want to make it up to you guys," said Jennifer. "I'll teach you how to juggle and how to balance—anything." She grinned.

"Hey, I'm sorry you had to stay in the hospital. And we're sorry you have all these problems with your family. Aren't we?" Dawn offered cheerfully.

Everyone shouted, "Yes!"

"Look. We stick together no matter how crazy our families are," said Angela.

"So don't ever be afraid to tell us what's going on with you," added Sonya.

Jennifer smiled. "I won't. Thanks, you guys."

Terri grinned. "What're we waiting for?"

They all climbed on their bikes and inched their front tires up to the starting line, which was a strip of masking tape stretched across the road.

Linda glanced over at the other racers, and her heart did a flip. Zack was racing, too! He'd brought a bunch of boys with him to make up a team. Then she noticed Celia had a team as well.

"I'm scared, Lin," Jennifer whispered as she hunched over the handlebars.

"You'll be fine, Jen," said Linda, reassuring her. "There are no cars on this road, remember that. The police blocked it off. We all just ride up and down this road. Nothing's going to happen to you."

She gave her friend a thumbs-up sign. Jennifer nodded nervously. Monique shot a cap gun. They were off!

Linda pedaled ahead furiously. As usual, Terri took an early lead, but Zack quickly caught up with her. Celia came up behind Zack and overtook him.

Linda stopped concentrating for a moment. She watched to see if Zack watched Celia. But he didn't. By that time Linda had dropped back a couple of places, so she pedaled fast to catch up.

Onlookers screamed as the racers got to the end of the block and turned to go back. Jennifer inched ahead of Angela, Sonya, Linda, Celia, Zack, and Terri. Terri glanced over at Jennifer as she passed her by. Jennifer kept up her lead and screamed over the finish line at least a bike length ahead of Terri.

The crowd went wild. When Linda rode across the finish line she jumped off her bike and gave Jennifer a big hug.

"We won! Our team won because of you, Jen!" she cried.

Jennifer's face lit up with a big smile. "We did, didn't we?"

"Congratulations, Jennifer!" cried Angela and Sonya, wrapping their arms around her.

Monique shouted as loudly as she could, "And the winner is—Jennifer Soo's team!" She walked over to Jennifer and placed a big box of chocolates in her hands. Then she pinned a blue ribbon on each team member's sweatshirt.

Zack, who came in second, came over to congratulate her,

too. Monique was already hugging Jennifer and forgot to give Zack and his team their red ribbons.

Celia rode up to the list of entrants, which was tied onto a cyclone fence. Then she walked over to Jennifer. "I didn't see your name on the list of entrants. So it's not fair that you've won."

"She was a last-minute replacement for Dawn, who almost got killed because of you!" declared Linda hotly.

"You're accusing me because that twerp fell off her bike?" Celia said with a little laugh.

Jennifer grabbed Celia's purple jean jacket from the cyclone fence and started going through the pockets.

"Hey, you stop that!" cried Celia. "That's breaking and entering."

"No, it isn't," replied Linda. "It's called frisking."

A tube of contact cement dropped onto the pavement. Celia swooped down to pick it up, but Linda was faster.

"Aha!" cried Dawn excitedly. "So that's who wrecked my bike."

"Linda did it," said Celia.

"She did not," Jennifer said in a loud voice.

Everyone was so surprised to hear from her, they turned around to stare.

"I didn't know there was glue in the can, and I handed it to Linda to use. We both thought there was oil in the can, which would've made the bikes work more smoothly," she explained.

"Nobody—except Celia—knew there was glue in the can until Dawn fell off the bike," said Linda, glaring at Celia.

Terri leveled her most poisonous glance at Celia.

"Polly did it," said Celia.

"I did not!" cried Polly.

Sonya just stood and slowly shook her head.

"We should call the police on you, Celia," said Monique.

"I'd like to glue your hands behind your back," said Terri through gritted teeth. She brandished the tube of glue at Celia threateningly.

Celia backed away from everybody, hugging her jean jacket. "Hey, you guys, I'm sorry, okay? I'm sorry Dawn got hurt. I was wrong."

"Wrong?" repeated the girls, looking from one to the other.

"Did I hear right?" asked Terri. "Celia actually admitted she was wrong?"

"Yes. I promise I'll never do anything like that again," Celia stated, sticking her chin in the air as though she was royalty.

"I don't believe it," cried Angela.

"Now I've heard everything," said Linda.

"Maybe she's turning over a new leaf," Dawn said hopefully.

"Let's not get carried away," said Terri, frowning at Celia.

"You must pay Dawn for the damage," said Linda.

"You can send me the bill, Dawn," Celia told her. "Now, are you all satisfied?"

"No," a voice piped up, belonging to Zack. "Monique, when do I get my ribbon?"

Monique turned bright red. "Oh, I'm sorry, Zack." She ran over to the cardboard box. Then she made a big ceremony out of pinning the ribbon to his chest. "And the second-place winner of the team bike race is—Zack—uh, what's your last name?"

"Schulman," he said, grinning.

"Sorry about that," said Monique. "Zack Schulman's team."

"Speech!" yelled Linda.

Zack put his palm across his chest and deadpanned, "This is the most exciting moment of my life, and I'm glad you all can share it with me—"

The other kids on his team giggled.

"And this is the most embarrassing moment of my life," murmured Monique. "Imagine, not knowing Zack's name!"

"Don't worry," said Linda brightly. "There are worse things that can happen."

"Come on. We have to judge the tricycle race," urged Dawn. She took off and rounded up the little kids. The crowd followed her.

After all the races had been run and everyone was leaving Zack came over to say goodbye to Linda.

"This was a lot of fun," he said. "I'm glad I came. Whose idea was it to have a bike race, anyway?"

Linda blushed. "Mine."

"I think you're pretty creative," he told her, grinning. "Well, 'bye."

"Goodbye," said Linda. When she turned around he shouted out, "Hey, Linda! Do you have a phone number?"

Hastily she dug in her pockets for a slip of paper to write on. She found a sales slip and wrote on the back of it.

"I'll call you," he said, waving as he got on his bike.

Linda nearly floated over to join the others.

"What was that all about?" asked Angela, who never missed a romantic moment.

Linda told them all what had happened.

"Watch out. This means Linda will be camped out next to the telephone for the next week," said Sonya, giggling.

"What if he loses my number?" asked Linda.

"We'll have to have another bike race so he can find you

again!" suggested Angela. "Or you can go to his uncle's bike shop."

Dawn sat down with the cigar box full of money that they had collected from the various events. She began to count. They had exactly ninety-three dollars.

"If we split it seven ways, it gives us each thirteen dollars and twenty-eight cents," said Dawn.

"Not enough for a pair of shoes," groaned Linda miserably.

"Linda, you can have my share," offered Jennifer, putting her hand on Linda's arm. "It was my fault it happened, and I didn't help with the contest much."

"You only won the race for us, kiddo," said Terri, slapping her on the back.

"Look, I think we should all pitch in our share of the money for the shoes," suggested Dawn.

"I think so, too," said Monique.

"The shoes cost about fifty dollars," said Linda.

"They'll be more with tax," said Angela.

"And they might cost more now," Sonya pointed out. "Your mom might have bought them on sale. You never know."

"She's right," said Dawn.

"This means none of you will get hardly anything out of the bike race," Linda told them.

"We get to help you," said Monique.

Linda felt her eyes fill up with tears. "I don't know how to thank you guys," she said. "You're lifesavers."

Jennifer and Dawn wrapped their arms around her first. The others followed their example.

"Hey, we're best friends, remember?" said Angela.

Chapter Twelve

⚘

Linda glanced at her watch worriedly. "I've got to run. I'll see you guys later."

"Goodbye, and good luck!" cried Dawn.

Jennifer hurried along beside Linda. "Where are you going?" she asked.

"To buy my mom's shoes," she answered, straddling her bike. "I want to get downtown before the store closes."

"Let me come," Jennifer pleaded, jumping on her bike. "I want to help."

Linda grinned. "Thanks. It'll be fun having you along, Jen."

The two girls rode down to the department store together.

Linda looked at the sign on the door of the store. "Fifteen minutes until closing time. Let's hurry!" she cried, parking her bike next to a tree.

Inside the store the two girls looked through the entire ladies' shoe department for the gold shoes.

"I don't see them anywhere. What if they're out of them?" exclaimed Linda.

"May I help you?" asked a saleswoman.

Linda was staring at a wall of shoes. "I'm looking for gold satin shoes in size eight," she said.

"I think an eight is a little big for you, dear," she said kindly.

"No, they're for my mom, not me," replied Linda quickly. "Please, I must find them. It's an emergency."

The saleswoman looked amused. "It's not often we have an emergency shoe problem."

Linda went on to describe the shoes in greater detail while following the saleswoman around.

"I never knew there were this many shoes in the entire world," said Jennifer. "It sure is confusing."

"Did you look on our sale rack?" asked the saleswoman.

"No. Where is it?" Of course, her mom shopped on sale racks whenever possible. Linda made a beeline for the sale rack.

She located her mother's size and scanned the racks for the shoes. Nothing.

"Wait!" Suddenly Jennifer dove to the floor and scrambled underneath the shoe rack. The rack began teetering dangerously, and shoes began to wobble.

"Girls, please!" cried the saleswoman, rushing to Linda's side. She gasped when she saw Jennifer underneath the rack. "Get out from under there this instant!"

Linda grabbed the side of the rack to hold it steady while Jennifer eased herself out from under it.

She hopped to her feet, carrying in one hand one gold satin shoe exactly like Mrs. Carmichael's fudge-stained ones. "Size eight!" crowed Jennifer triumphantly. "And they're only twenty-five dollars and ninety-five cents!"

The saleswoman wore a horrified look on her face. "I'm really glad to hear it."

"Whew! Oh, Jen, this is wonderful," Linda said with relief. "But where's the other shoe?"

"We keep the matching shoe in the back room," explained the saleswoman. "I'll get it for you. Just promise me you won't get into any more trouble while I'm gone." She frowned at the girls.

Linda and Jennifer tried very hard not to start giggling as the saleswoman bustled off to find the mate to the shoe.

"This reminds me of the old days," said Jennifer. "Except we're not doing anything bad."

"Shhh!" Linda warned. "Don't even mention it."

Jennifer giggled. "The shoe rack might be bugged."

Just then the saleswoman returned with a box containing both shoes. Linda nearly melted with relief.

"You don't know how happy this makes me," she told the saleswoman. She began to tell the story of the fudgy shoes. The woman nodded with disbelief.

Jennifer pulled out her wallet and placed two twenty-dollar bills on the counter.

"What're you doing, Jen?" asked Linda. "I've got the money."

"Let me pay for them," Jennifer insisted. "Listen, my mom sent me some extra spending money, plus my bike-race money. I'm really sorry about what I did."

The saleswoman rang up the sale and handed a pink shoe bag to Linda. They were the last customers to leave the store before it was locked up.

"You're forgiven, Jen. And thanks. But I don't want you to use all your money. It's the thought that counts," she said, handing Jennifer's spending money back to her. "Besides, the shoes were cheaper than we expected. Come on. Let's go get a sundae to celebrate."

Jennifer looked down at her sneakers, and both girls laughed.

"This time I'm not going to let you wear the sundae on your shoes!" cried Linda.

Linda presented the shoes to her mother the minute she and Jennifer arrived home.

"Mom!" she cried, bursting through the door.

"Surprise!" added Jennifer.

Mrs. Carmichael was reading, and her book fell into her lap. "What?" she asked in confusion.

Linda sat down beside her and handed her the shoebox.

Mrs. Carmichael smiled and lifted the lid. The she folded back the tissue and lifted the shoes out. "Oh, my. Aren't they beautiful? Thank you so much, Linda." She leaned over and kissed the top of Linda's head.

Linda grinned. "You're welcome, Mom. Jennifer helped."

"Thank you, Jennifer," said Mrs. Carmichael, surprised. "You didn't have to do that."

Jennifer blushed. "Well, Mrs. Carmichael, it was my fault your shoes got ruined. I made these great hot fudge sundaes for Linda and myself, and I dropped mine on top of your shoes, and . . ."

Mrs. Carmichael made a funny face. "I'm not sure I want to know what my shoes were doing near a hot fudge sundae. But I do want to know why you didn't tell me this earlier, Jennifer. And why you covered up for her, Linda."

"Jennifer was afraid you would send her home, Mom," Linda explained. Then Jennifer told Mrs. Carmichael what was happening at home.

"I'm so sorry, Jennifer," Mrs. Carmichael said, giving Jennifer a squeeze. "This must be very painful for you. I hope we can help you in some way." Then she turned to Linda. "I'm sorry for being so hard on you, Linda. Now that I know what happened, I can see you're very trustworthy. If I were Jennifer, I'd be glad to have you as my friend."

Linda and Jennifer grinned at each other. "I'm very glad," said Jennifer.

"Thanks, Mom," said Linda, hugging her.

Mrs. Carmichael put on her shoes and sighed with contentment. "I'm so happy. Now I can go to that wedding tomorrow in style."

Linda nudged Jennifer. "See? I told you she was easygoing."

"We have money left over from the bike race," said Linda as she emptied a bag of chocolate chips into a bowl of batter the next day.

The Carmichaels' kitchen was the scene of a big cookie-making session.

"And I have some spending money from my mom," added Jennifer.

Dawn scooped dough onto her finger. "Wow, we should go on a shopping spree."

"Where shall we go? The mall?" asked Sonya. "I want new barrettes."

"We could go to the movies," suggested Monique.

Suddenly the phone rang. Jon called out, "Hey, Jen, it's for you!"

She skipped over to the phone. Both her parents were on the other end.

Linda watched her friend. Finally Jennifer got off the phone, wearing a big smile.

"Guess what, everybody?"

"You're not moving," guessed Angela.

"My mom is getting transferred to Warren Hill," said Jennifer.

"That's near Gladstone!" cried Linda with excitement.

"I know. She said we can live in Gladstone. I'm going home in a few days, but I'll be back in the fall," Jennifer explained.

"Hey, that's fabulous," said Sonya. "What about your dad?"

Jennifer's expression fell. "He's staying in L.A., and I'll get to visit him sometimes."

"That's better news than you expected," Angela pointed out.

"I'm happy for you," Monique said.

"Moving is hard, Jennifer. And divorce is harder," said Sonya knowledgeably. "But it's worked out okay for me."

"Me, too," said Angela. "Even though I wish my mom would have a really good romance."

Dawn patted Jennifer's hand with her floury hands. "I'm so glad you'll be here next year."

Jennifer bit down on a cookie. "I already have friends in my new home!"

"You sure do. You've got an entire club," Angela told her, giving her a big hug.

"Welcome to the High Visibility Club!" exclaimed Linda.

The girls tumbled over one another to give Jennifer a big welcoming hug.

The phone rang again. Linda gasped and ran to answer it. Everybody shouted, "Zack!"

About the Author

SUSAN SMITH was born in Great Britain and has lived most of her life in California and New York. She began writing when she was thirteen years old and has authored a number of novels for teenagers, including the Samantha Slade series by Archway Paperbacks. She is currently living in Santa Fe, New Mexico, with her two children. Both children have provided her with many ideas and observations that she has included in her books. In addition to writing, Ms. Smith enjoys travel, horseback riding, skiing, and swimming.

Look for Best Friends #10:

Sonya and the Haunting of Room 16A

coming in October 1990

Sonya loves everything about junior high except science, where her seventh-grade class is assigned to dissect frogs. To make matters worse, someone is letting live frogs loose in the classroom! At the school Halloween carnival, frogs ruin the cakewalk in room 16A, sending kids screaming in all directions. Sonya and her friends are determined to find out just who is responsible for this ''hoppy'' Halloween!